Claiming Family

ELEMENTUM GENUS

BOOK 2

DESI LIN

COVEY PUBLISHINGA

CLAIMING FAMILY

COVEY PUBLISHING, LLC

Published by Covey Publishing, LLC

PO Box 550219, Gastonia, NC 28055-0219

Cover Design Copyright © 2020 Covey

Book Design by Covey, www.coveypublishing.com

Copy Editing by Covey Publishing, LLC

Printed in the United States of America.

First Printing, 2020

Elementum Genus

Claiming Flame

Claiming Family

Angel Falls

Saving Him

For K. – You keep me going when I want to give up. Love you.

ACKNOWLEDGMENTS

This book put me through the ringer and I nearly gave up on it several times. Thankfully I had a lot of support and encouragement that kept me at it, even through trashing a half written book three times.

Lyn at Covey always ready for a question, complaint or even a rant about how the damn characters weren't cooperating, again. The Rebels, who read through countless sections of text to help me figure out how to make the story right. My family who suffered through many a rushed dinner or a frantic mom. As always K, without whom I swear I would have tossed in the towel ages ago.

Most importantly, you my readers. You have been patient while I struggled to bring you the best story I could. Thanks for sticking with me.

ONE

A mild breeze ruffled my bright-red hair as I stood, trembling, on the white front porch. Warmth radiated through the long-sleeved, sequined, black shirt I wore. The hand at the small of my back reminded me I wasn't facing this alone.

"You're fine, beautiful." Brooks' warm breath ghosted over my ear as one of his blond curls tickled my cheek. "We're right here, no matter what."

His words radiated through me, settling into my core like the truth I wanted them to be. Things between us were still so new and tentative, the Iunctura only two weeks old.

My eyes traveled over the boys who refused to let

me push them away. JJ caught my eyes with his own golden ones and winked, his black hair brushed back from his face. Souta's rich brown-black hair fell over his forehead as he blew me a kiss, the dark pools of his eyes sparkling with mischief. I tilted my head to catch Brooks' blue gaze.

Knowing they were here made me stronger, and they kept showing me they wanted to be there for me. Despite my desire to find my father, fear made me drag my feet. The boys's gentle encouragement helped me conquer the fear.

"What if he hates me?" I whispered, eyes fixated on the plain, white door.

"No one could hate you, hot stuff." Souta's hand squeezed mine tightly.

I found the grasp reassuring and clung to it like a lifeline as I shook.

JJ's arm snaked around my waist. "Listen, firefly, whatever you want, whatever happens, you always have us."

Oh, how I wanted to believe those words. Still, the tension of what I was about to do slid away at my guys's touch. I leaned back into Brooks' chest as Souta and JJ moved closer, our bodies all touching. They were my strength, confidence, and courage.

JJ held my hand through every step of the search when I wanted to let my fear stop me. Brooks decided to call May when we hit block after block. When I couldn't decide if I wanted to come today, Souta took my hand and guided me into the car. I wouldn't be here without them.

Taking a deep breath, I knocked.

After a minute, the door opened. A slight woman with wavy, brown hair and mildly exotic features smiled curiously at us.

"Hello. Can I help you?" Her almond-shaped, hazel eyes sparkled with curiosity as they traveled over us, the corners of her mouth quirking up into a puzzled smile. The natural tan of her skin highlighted the emerald-green blouse she wore paired with simple dark-wash jeans.

I couldn't talk. I don't know what I expected, but not this stunning woman. A glint caught my eye, and my gaze drifted down, finding the modest diamond set in gold on her finger. Fear tore through me, freezing me on the spot, unable to do anything more than stare and tremble.

"Sorry to disturb you, ma'am." JJ stepped forward. "We're looking for Michael Phoenix?"

I held my breath as I waited for her response. A

hand cupped the back of my neck, and I leaned into the comforting gesture.

"Then, you came to the right place. Hang on." She turned her head and hollered into the house. "Michael, honey, the door is for you."

An unintelligible response rumbled from deeper in the house, and a minute later a man came to the door. Shock ran through me. His hair, the same as my natural brown before I dyed it red, and his brown eyes mirrored my own. Tall and lean, he wore a fire department T-shirt. I always believed I inherited my looks from my mother, but as I stared at this man, my father, I realized where they actually came from.

His smile held a bit of confusion as he took us in. "Hi."

I swallowed and forced myself to talk, the hand still holding mine giving a quick, encouraging squeeze. "Hi, my name is Seraphina Embers." His eyes widened in what might be recognition at my last name. "And I, um, well…" I thrust the letter from my mother out to him. "Here." I'd reread it several times over the last two weeks, so the words filled my mind as his eyes scanned the well-creased letter.

His head jerked up, eyes wide with shock. "You're my daughter?"

I couldn't read his mood, but I nodded, trying to

lift my hand to pick at my cuticles before remembering Souta's firm grip on my hand. "It seems like it."

The woman who answered the door came up to stand at his side and rested a hand on his arm. I feared she might be angry, and though her surprise showed, her wide eyes held no malice. She smiled sweetly at me.

"Michael? You have a daughter?" Confusion laced her voice.

"I had no idea I had a daughter," Michael whispered as he shook his head.

The woman next to him chuckled. "I guess we should ask her and her friends in?" Her tone made it a question.

"What?" Michael glanced down at her, startled, then at me. "Yes, yes. Come in, Seraphina. It seems we have a lot to talk about. Kelly, can you call Ash?"

Michael stepped back to invite us in, but I didn't get across the threshold before I found myself enveloped in a huge bear hug.

"A daughter. Wow." The words were little more than a breath, but I still heard them.

With the boys, I was slowly beginning to get used to casual touch. They were constantly touching me in little ways, a hug, an arm slung over the shoulder, a hand squeeze. With others, though, casual touch remained uncomfortable for me. I managed not to stiffen when Michael hugged me, but I pulled away quickly without returning it.

Michael smiled ruefully as he led us into a comfortable, casually decorated living room. A worn, chocolate brown couch dominated most of the small room. A matching armchair, dark wood coffee table and matching end tables, a couple dark-wood bookshelves, and a pair of simple brass lamps completed the room.

On the walls and bookcases, a few scattered picture frames showed Michael and the woman who answered the door, who even now hovered uncertainly. A couple contained a young boy, while one showed the boy older. The aura of comfort and family permeated everything.

What was I doing here? I didn't belong here; I wasn't part of a family. I didn't know how to act or what Michael might expect of me.

I wanted to run.

"Michael," the tremble in the woman's voice told me I wasn't alone in my uncertainty, "I'm going to find some refreshments and call Ash." Her slim, elegant hand fidgeted with the seam of her dark-wash jeans.

The smile Michael turned her way practically glowed with love and adoration.

I swallowed and glanced at the boys. They didn't look at me that way, but I hoped someday they might. We weren't in any hurry.

"Seraphina, this is my fiancée, Kelly." Michael wrapped an arm around her waist and pressed a kiss to her lips. "Thank you, sweetheart," he murmured to her, releasing his hold so she could head into the kitchen.

I watched the whole exchange, a host of emotions running rampant inside me. A hand at my back made me glance over my shoulder. Brooks smiled at me. I took a deep breath, reassured by the presence of my boys, and moved to sit on the couch.

Naturally, the boys surrounded me.

Michael's assessing gaze reminded me I had yet to introduce the boys. "Um, this is Brooks, Souta, and JJ. My, um, Genus."

I wasn't entirely comfortable revealing our dating status when I didn't know how this man would react to having me thrust into his life.

"I don't know quite where to start," Michael said as he sank into the armchair. With my hand freed, I picked at my cuticles.

My nightmares were filled with images of him

throwing the letter at me and slamming the door in my face. To sit in his comfortable living room filled with warmth and family left me floundering.

"So, it's true?" I kept expecting him to deny it, to throw us out, to demand more proof.

Once again, reading my mind, Brooks' hand cupped the back of my neck.

Michael still held the letter, and he glanced at it again, blinking several times and sighing. "I've no reason to believe otherwise." Though steady, Michael spoke slowly and softly. "Calista, your mother, didn't like lies. She would never write it down if she didn't believe it to be true, and it's her handwriting."

Michael looked up from the letter at the soft shuffle of footsteps, smiling wide again as Kelly rejoined us. On the coffee table, she set a tray of glasses, filled with ice, and a pitcher of lemonade, indicating for us to help ourselves as she perched on the arm of the chair Michael sat in. As I poured a drink, I didn't pay attention to the plate on the tray, my stomach too busy churning to think about eating.

Catching my gaze, Michael smiled. "By the way, when's your birthday?"

"I turned eighteen a couple of weeks ago." I licked my lips and gulped down some lemonade in the hopes of quenching the desert my throat became.

Michael nodded as if it made perfect sense, though sense of what, I didn't know. "I see. The timing would be right. We'll do a DNA test to be sure, but I really can't doubt what I see with my own eyes." He grinned at me.

I tried to smile back, but I'm sure it looked more like a grimace. Butterflies erupted in my stomach. No, wait, not butterflies. More like bats or, I don't know, flying monkeys?

After we'd sat in tense silence for a minute or two, a hand wrapped around mine, and JJ drew my hand into his lap, his thumb running across my palm. "Firefly, did you have questions?"

"I, um, I…" Questions ran rampant in my head.

They'd been there since I first read the letter, and now, when I finally had the ability to get all the answers I ever wanted, I couldn't get a single one past my lips. I simply stared at the face so much like my own.

"You might wonder why I never sought you out?" Michael offered. "Until today, this letter, I didn't know you existed. I can't imagine how things have been for you. Please know, if I had any idea you existed, I would have moved heaven and earth to find you."

I bit my lip, unsure how to feel or respond. Most people would be thrilled to hear that, wouldn't they?

Except for the incident with Aguirre, things hadn't been too bad for me. I was lonely and didn't realizing how much I wanted to belong somewhere, until the guys shoved their way into my life, but still not bad. Plenty of people were worse off than me. Though, I couldn't deny how much having a father would have meant.

Lost in my thoughts and worries, I failed to notice Souta until he scooped me up just enough to sit in my spot and settle me into his lap.

"You can do this, hot stuff. We're right here," Souta murmured into my hair.

I restrained the sudden need to stiffen. Sitting in a lap went beyond the casual touch I'd come to accept from them, but then JJ and Brooks rested their hands on me. My whole being relaxed.

When I looked back at Michael and Kelly, I noticed Kelly's confused gaze. Outside of Elementum marked places, the boys and I drew up a plan so we wouldn't draw too much attention or questions. None of us thought anything of our actions in the home of another Elementum, but we failed to consider whether Kelly was an Elementum or not.

"Who are you boys again? And what is your

relationship with Seraphina?" She asked, only genuine curiosity in her voice.

I admired her easy calm and composure.

The front door slammed open before anyone could answer Kelly's question.

A young man, a couple years older than me by the looks of things, strode into the room. Average height, slender build, and the same ash-brown hair, highlighted with blond in his case, told me he must be Michael's son. Which made him my brother. Also, he walked in as if he owned the place.

"Hey, Dad. What's going on?" He glanced quickly in our direction but seemed to dismiss us.

I picked at my cuticle again until JJ rested a hand over mine, stilling the nervous action. A father, stepmother, and brother? I expected one person, a father, and didn't know how to act or even feel about a full-fledged family.

I should be thrilled, right? Instead, fear took over, looping through my mind. What if I wasn't good enough? What if I said or did the wrong thing? What if they wanted more than I could give them? Would they like the person I was? Who would they expect me to be? How would they expect me to act?

I reached for one of the small, buttery looking cookies Kelly brought out when she rejoined us, hoping to distract myself from these useless thoughts. I'd seen this type of cookie a million times before, small with sparkly white sugar on top in intricate designs. I'd tasted them only once before, though, the day May told me the Richmonds would no longer be my family.

The memory slammed into me like a truck, one I'd long ago buried and forgotten.

Tara and Mark rushed around the house. Tara wore the frilly apron she only used when doing fancy baking. I loved her apron. I'd gotten in trouble for wearing it just two days before. Tara told me the apron was her special one, and it needed to be nice for when company came.

I watched through the second-floor slats as Tara straightened cushions and vacuumed floors, putting the living room in company-ready condition. My stomach growled when I noticed the tray of fancy-looking cookies. Different from anything she'd put out for company in the past, I felt sure she didn't bake them. The smell of Tara's fancy baking usually lingered in the air, but it wasn't present now.

The doorbell rang, and I strained to see who it might be. Tara often invited friends for tea parties, and she'd promised I could join them next time. A hand clamped down on my shoulder as Mark squatted beside me, smiling.

"Stay here, Seraphina, until you're called for. This is a very important meeting for Tara and me." He spoke softly and brushed a lock of my waist-length, ash-brown hair away from my face.

I grinned as I nodded. I loved the way my entire name rolled fluidly off his tongue, Tara's as well. I felt like a princess when they said it.

Mark rose and headed downstairs as Tara led Maybelle into the living room.

I cocked my head to the side, watching curiously. Maybelle didn't visit often, and Mark said it was important. I desperately wanted to go down, especially when my stomach growled again. Mark and Tara both seemed sad. Tara's shoulders drooped as she leaned heavily into Mark and spoke quietly to Maybelle. Tara placed a hand to her stomach, and I worried she might be sick.

Tara and Mark were the only parents I knew, though they often spoke about my birth mother. I didn't know what would happen to me if they were gone. I chewed my lip as I watched them. Maybelle's face grew ever more serious as they spoke, then her eyes drifted up to find me sitting at the balcony railing of the second floor.

She turned back to Tara and Mark, nodding.

When they rose and left the living room, I stood, wondering what was going on.

Maybelle looked back up at me. "Come on down, sweetheart. I need to talk to you."

I hadn't learned yet how awful that phrase was, but I was about to.

I hurried downstairs, hair flying out behind me as I ran. I snitched up three of the fancy-looking cookies on my way to plop onto the couch. The buttery, sugary goodness of the cookies only seemed to whet my appetite, and I grabbed three more as Maybelle began talking.

"I've been given some... news." Maybelle hesitated, then patted my knee. "Tara and Mark, they, well, they're going to have a baby."

I bounced excitedly at the news. A baby! I would have a little brother or sister, not real of course, but as close as I'd get. The heavy sigh Maybelle released stopped my bouncing.

"I know it sounds like great news, and it is. For a very long time, they believed they'd never be able to have children. They were told so many times. It was why they were willing to take you."

The serious expression on her face made me want to bite my lip again. Instead, I picked at my nails, needing to do something.

"Tara is going to have a hard time for the next

several months, and having an active, energetic five-year-old around won't be a good idea."

I froze, something inside me going cold. Maybelle picked me up and settled me in her lap, arms going around me to pull me close. I stiffened, unwilling to be comforted, waiting for rest.

"It means she won't be able to take care of you anymore." Though quiet, the words fell like bricks on my ears.

"No," I whispered the words, my hands going to my ears, knowing what the next words would be. "No, no, no, no, no." My eyes burned as my voice rose.

"We're going to pack up your things. Clothes and a few of your favorite toys, and, for now, I'm going to take you to the school you're starting in a couple of days." Her soft voice, meant to be reassuring, only made me colder.

My eyes overflowed, and the tears ran down my cheeks. Maybelle tried to cuddle me close, but I remained stiff and unyielding. Quick, short breaths heaved my chest, and the cookies, so delicious a short time ago, churned in my stomach.

Why? Why was I being forced to leave? Didn't they love me anymore? What did I do wrong? I shook.

"No!" I screamed, tears and snot pouring down my face. "I didn't do anything bad! I'll be better! I promise!" My tiny fists beat at Maybelle's chest.

Warm hands stroked my hair, incoherent murmurs working their way inside me. I refused to let it calm me down. My world crumbled around me, and nothing would make it better. Maybelle picked me up as she stood, securing an arm under my butt. I buried my head in her shoulder.

"Here are her things." Tara's gentle voice made me lift my head. She stood at the door, a beat-up, blue suitcase at her feet and Mr. Snuggles, my favorite, floppy-eared bunny in her hand. She held out Mr. Snuggles with a sad smile. "I'm so sorry, sweetheart."

I snatched Mr. Snuggles and cuddled him close, the familiar scent pouring into my nostrils. My oldest possession, he'd been with me as long as I could remember. Tara told me she'd bought it the day Maybelle asked about my coming to live with them. I'd always seen it as a symbol of her love. Something soured inside me, and anger burned away my tears.

"You said you loved me!" I screamed. "You lied! I hate you!" I threw Mr. Snuggles at Tara. He bounced off her chest and fell at her feet. Maybelle leaned down, one hand keeping me secured, the other grabbing the suitcase. Tara sighed and bent to pick up Mr. Snuggles. She held the bunny out to me, but I didn't take it.

"I don't want it!" I screamed at her. "I don't want it! I hate you! I hate you! I hate you!"

Tara shifted and handed the bunny to Maybelle. "She'll want it when she quits being angry."

I wouldn't want it. I hated it. I hated everything to do with them. My tears dried on my face as I glared at Tara. "I hate you." I hissed at her as the door creaked open.

"I know, honey." She smiled sadly and turned away as we walked to the car.

The front door closed, and the last of my hope died.

"What the fuck do you mean, she's my sister?"

The harsh shout yanked me out of the resurfaced memory.

I started, reflexively squeezing the hand gripping mine. Disoriented and disturbed by what I'd remembered, I sucked in a fast breath. My eyes darted around the room to figure out what happened while lost in my own head. The guy who burst in, stood nearly nose-to-nose with Michael, brows drawn together, arms folded over his chest, mouth turned down in a cross between a frown and a sneer.

"Ashton Michael Phoenix!" Michael didn't yell, he didn't need to. If he'd been addressing me in the stern, I'll-take-no-shit voice he used, I'd shut up and listen. "You will calm down, and we will talk about this."

"No fucking way! You don't get to drop this on me and expect me to be calm!" Ashton bellowed at Michael. He spun and thrust a finger at me. "Look at her! She can't be more than a couple years younger than me!"

His anger shook me to the core, and I scrunched tight into Souta, his arms wrapping around me and squeezing. When Ashton stalked toward me, JJ stood from his seat next to us, and Brooks came around the couch to block me from the irate guy.

Their protectiveness helped ease my fear and caused me to feel a little silly. What was I doing? This wasn't like me; I didn't do shrinking violet. Although, I never had to worry about familial relationships before, part of me wanted to snarl at him, but a voice inside kept whispering, worrying about Michael's reaction if I did.

Until the moment I learned my father might still be living, I'd always believed I didn't need family. In my search for him, my emotions kept changing, bouncing back and forth like a yoyo between excitement and fear. It took standing on his doorstep, staring at the entrance for me to realize how much I wanted—needed—him to accept me. I needed to have a relationship with this man and, now, with my brother. The problem? I didn't know the first thing about being a family.

"Just how old are you anyway?" Ashton spat the words at me, eyes hard and cold, body taut, mouth set in a thin line.

"None of your business," JJ shot right back at him. "Try not being a total asshole, and maybe she'll tell you."

I placed a hand at JJ's back to get his attention.

He glanced back at me, nodded, then slid to the side.

"I turned eighteen a couple weeks ago, and I'd appreciate it if you'd lower your voice, please." Calm, firm, and to the point seemed best for the situation, but Ashton ignored me as he spun back to Michael.

"Three years." His voice shook, but not from tears or sadness. His fists clenched at his side. "Three years, Dad?" His volume rose as he spoke. "Three fucking years, Dad!"

My eyes widened at the pure rage emanating from him, the air so heavy I almost choked on it. It seemed like there was more here than I understood. Ashton's reaction to me was too extreme.

Michael leaned over to Kelly, whispering in her ear. She nodded, picked up the tray of cookies, and left the room. I felt like we should leave quietly, too. I began to unfurl, but Michael caught my eye. "Stay, please." I sank back down, still uncertain we should be there.

"Was Mom even cold, yet? Did you bury her first? Or were you busy screwing some whore instead?" Ashton's loud accusation echoed in the room.

By the way Michael's face instantly shuttered, Ash had gone too far. "I loved your mother more than my own life." Michael's calm and quiet statement scared me more than anything else. "I think it's time for you go home, Ashton."

The two of them stared at each other, a clash of wills taking place before our eyes.

After a moment, Ashton spun and stormed toward the door. He stopped at the couch, gaze fixed firmly ahead but his words meant for me. "You are not my sister," he said flatly. "I will never accept that."

As I watched him stride to the door, slamming it behind him, something inside me cracked. From the immediate reaction of the guys, I must have telegraphed my feelings. They each rubbed some section of me gently. I swatted at their hands gently, the feel of them too much to handle at that moment, then unfurled myself from Souta's lap. Standing, I crossed my arms over my stomach, unsure of how to respond to the situation.

Michael rubbed his eyes and sighed. "I'm sorry you had to witnessed that, Seraphina," Michael said as he came toward me. "Ash tends to explode first and ask questions later. He'll come around."

I nodded, not sure what else to do. Michael's smile seemed sad. I impulsively wanted to hug him, but I held back.

"I'd like you to have my number, and I'm going to give you Ash's as well. You may find yourself needing it."

Pulling my phone from my pocket, I handed it to him, and he plugged in the numbers. When he finished, he held it out to me. After grabbing it and sliding it into my pocket, I took a step back, nearly tripping over Brooks as his arm wrapped around my waist. "We should take Sera home."

"It was nice to meet you," I whispered. I hated my timid reaction, but I couldn't seem to stop myself from doing it. We turned and headed to the door, JJ and Souta following us.

"Seraphina," Michael called out to us as Brooks opened the door. I glanced back at him. "Please don't let my son's actions make you think ill of us. I'd like to get to know you, to be a father to you."

Emotion swelled in my throat, making speaking impossible. Instead, I nodded again.

As we said our goodbyes and Brooks ushered me out the door, it occurred to me I never asked Michael to call me Sera. No one had called me Seraphina since I'd left Tara and Mark. I'd never wanted to hear my full name again. But for some reason, hearing it from Michael felt right.

TWO

As the car glided over the road, I leaned into JJ, needing his strength. Meeting Michael, remembering Mark and Tara, and rejection by my brother was an emotional roller coaster all tangled up, forming a knot in the pit of my stomach. I didn't know how to feel about any of it, and nothing felt real anymore.

Was this my life? Was that scared girl back there me? Why didn't I yell back or stand up for myself when Ash came at me like that? I wanted to go back and tell Michael I was better than that, I wasn't some frail little girl who'd be hurt by words said in anger and likely not meant.

JJ's arm snaked around me, pulling me close as he dropped a kiss on my forehead. With a sigh, I let my mind wander, hoping to distract myself from my internal mess of emotions.

I shifted in the seat, a twinge of pain darting through me, sending my thoughts to my former tormentor, Aguirre. Once I settled in at Souta's, my mind obsessed over trying to rationalize why she'd treated me the way she did.

Those answers came, eventually.

May was waiting for us when we arrived home from school, about a week after everything went down. She stood on the front porch, looking as elegant as ever. Her snow-white hair brushed away from her nearly unlined face and curled around her ears. A simple, black camisole and pants paired with a sheer orange and yellow, knee-length jacket with chunky gold jewelry highlighted her dark skin. Her eyes lacked their usual sparkle, though. My insides cramped at the blank expression on her face. I had never seen May without a smile.

"Hello, my dear," she greeted us as I stepped out of the car, hands with a death grip on the straps of my bag. Souta stepped up beside me, a hand pressing against the small of my back. "I have some news, regarding the recent events."

She meant Aguirre.

I hitched my backpack unnecessarily, a twinge of pain running up my sides from my still painful ribs. Souta noticed and wrapped a hand around the bag I'd stubbornly insisted I could handle just fine. I didn't resist as he slid it from my shoulder, then kissed my cheek. The boys did things like that more and more lately, little bits of affection I still wasn't entirely used to.

"I'll be inside if you need me." Souta's words whispered over my ear before he strode into the house.

I turned to May, uncertain if I even wanted to know what she came to tell me. Could anything explain away what that woman did? Could anything make it easier to move past? It didn't matter. I needed answers. They wouldn't take back what happened. They wouldn't help me move on. However, I needed to know. What would make someone behave that way?

"Let's walk, dear." May held a handout for me with a smile, then immediately pulled it back.

I didn't do a lot of casual touching, but the boys were getting me used to it. Shoving aside my discomfort, I reached over and took her hand. I felt like a little kid, but she only wanted to provide comfort.

She led us toward a red brick path, lined on either side with sweet-smelling, red cedar mulch. It wound its way around to the side of the house to a flower garden.

Neither of us spoke, simply walked along the path. A riot of colors spread out on either side of the path. Pinks and purples bordered by white, oranges and reds exploding from a sea of deep green. Each bed separated by simple, cedar wood pieces stacked two high, a work of art contributing to the beauty of the whole garden. A cool breeze made the taller flowers dance and brought the scent of recent rain wafting toward us.

We found a white iron bench sitting under a wooden arch with vibrant bluish-purple morning glories climbing the sides and settled down.

"I know nothing I'm about to tell you will make any difference for you, but I hope it gives you closure." May stared off into the distance. "It's taken time, and honestly, I still have trouble wrapping my head around it, but we finally have something resembling answers."

She shook her head and sighed as she turned toward me. "Apparently, there's history between your mother and Aguirre. We found a lot of convoluted memories and half stories, but suffice it to say, bad blood existed between them. From the things she's said and what we know, our current hypothesis is that when she heard who you were, she became determined to get revenge on your mother by making things as difficult as possible for you. Combined with her mental condition and the recent rapid deterioration…"

Her voice trailed off as she shook her head, the implication that I'd been the perfect target hovering between us.

"Her mental—"

May held up a hand to stop my question. "I don't know. Even for us, that information is privileged, with no exceptions for the Councilum. She's been seeing someone for a while now, we knew that much, but we don't know why she appears to be worsening so quickly. Since her attack on you and the evaluation of her mental state, she's been admitted to a local institution."

I had been right. Knowing didn't help anything. Her reasons for treating me the way she had were crap and bullshit. May didn't have to come here and tell me. I wasn't about to hurt her feelings for doing so. "Thanks for telling me."

May opened her arms for a hug, which I gave her, though I kept it short and swift. "I'm sorry to do this, sweetie, but I have to run. I need to stop by and see Tarin before I'm due to fly out again."

I only nodded. Being a Sage kept her busy.

"Call me if you need me, or just to say hello." She stood and took off back down the path, leaving me to ponder the absurdity of the situation.

. . .

"What's eating you, beautiful?" Brooks' deep, gentle rumble pulled me from my reverie. He reached between the front seats to stroke a finger down the side of my face.

I tried to smile, but heavy mental exhaustion settled over me, and I only managed to twitch the side of mouth up a couple millimeters.

"Nothing, I'm okay," I lied, my voice breathy and listless even to my own ears.

From the frown pulling down his full lips and the narrowing of his blue eyes, it was clear he wasn't accepting my words. He always seemed so in tune with my emotions and feelings. I kept forgetting that.

"Don't make her talk if she's not feeling it," JJ snapped, arm tightening around me.

I nudged him when the squeeze became just a touch too tight. His golden gaze darted down to me, and I tried to smile.

"It's okay." I sighed and buried my face in his chest, the short, neon-red strands of my hair falling to obscure my face.

"None of this is okay, hot stuff," Souta ground out between clenched teeth.

When I glanced at him in the driver's seat, his knuckles were nearly white from the strength of his grip on the steering wheel, and his usually well-groomed brown-black hair fell limply around his face.

I rolled my eyes slowly as I pushed away from JJ and shoved my hair out of my face. "Stop, you two." Reaching out, I took hold of Brooks' hand when he rested it against my cheek. "I'm just... I don't know... mentally wiped?"

Brooks laced our fingers together.

"I expected to meet my father today. I braced myself for that particular roller coaster. Instead of only my father, I got a possible stepmother and a brother thrust on me, one who wants... wants..." I choked on an unexpected sob.

Why did my throat suddenly tighten up? I tried to shake it off, along with the melancholy surrounding me.

"A brother who wants nothing to do with me," I finished in a rush. My chest tightened as my eyes burned. Closing them, I took a deep breath. "It's a lot to take in."

A hand stroked my hair, drawing my attention away from Brooks. JJ stared out the window at the city rushing by, one hand now resting against my neck, but he was obviously paying attention to what Brooks and I said.

I turned back to Brooks. "My mind just wants to shut down, I think."

The car slowed as Souta pulled into the drive leading to his house.

I took a deep breath, trying to hold back the exhausted sobs wanting to leak out. I hated them, wanted desperately to understand why they even existed, why my stomach still churned, my eyes still burned. Not going to happen right now, though.

Souta parked the car near the triple garage, then hopped out and opened my door.

The idea of walking all the way to my room exhausted me. I took in each of the guys standing around the curved driveway. Brooks with his blond curls tucked behind his ears, piercing blue eyes carried a laid-back attitude and style. Souta had flare with mouth quirked up in a flirty smile, dark eyes sparkling with mischievousness, brown-black hair now set back in place, a simple but perfectly coordinated outfit showing off his compact Asian build. JJ, my beautiful artist, shines through his gold eyes shimmering in the sun, black hair brushing the black leather jacket he wore over a white shirt with bright green and yellow splashes of color.

They would do anything for me. So, I did

something I never thought I would, thrusting out my bottom lip and whining.

They all chuckled.

"Come on, hot stuff." Souta shook his head. "If you get out of the car, I'll carry you upstairs, and Brooks will make you a malted milk."

A couple days after I officially moved in, I'd been craving a glass of chocolate milk in the middle of the night. Despite searching the fridge and every one of the many shelves in the extremely large pantry, I'd failed to find chocolate syrup. What I found instead was a container labeled chocolate malted milk. I'd never seen it before, but it said chocolate and looked like the powder I used on occasion.

As I returned to the kitchen to make a glass, Souta entered at the same time, caught sight of the container, and told me it tasted best blended. He made us both big glasses.

From the first sip, I was addicted. It tasted like chocolate milk, only better.

My whine turned to a purr as I climbed out of the car.

Souta laughed harder before he scooped me up, settling me against his strong chest.

JJ followed us into the house and upstairs while Brooks made for the kitchen.

I buried my head against Souta's shoulder, eyes heavy. They drifted close before snapping open again when the door to my room creaked open. My eyes grew heavy again as Souta laid me on the bed.

After a few minutes, the shuffle of steps forced my lids open just the tiniest bit to see Brooks placing a glass on the nightstand.

I rolled to my side and propped myself up, thankful he put a straw in the glass. The malted chocolate deliciousness didn't last long.

When I drank every last drop, I curled into the velvety softness of the covers, I barely noticed the guys' presence as I let darkness and oblivion take over.

THREE

The next week passed in a surreal fog. I moved through the day-to-day motions, going to class, eating, and washing on autopilot. I was still getting used to the room Souta's parents let me stay in; everything felt slightly off balance. Even though they'd told me I could change things to fit my tastes and to tell Shiro what I wanted, it felt wrong to change anything.

As a guest, it seemed prudent to remain as unobtrusive as possible.

My whole brain wanted to occupy itself by trying to analyze every detail of what happened at Michael's, every nuance of feeling, but the guys and I still needed to talk about what happened with the Iunctura on my birthday.

We'd only known each other a few weeks, not nearly enough time to develop any kind of friendship, let alone create the foundations for a lasting romantic involvement. And suddenly, these three men wanted a relationship with me, when I've never even had one boyfriend before? Heck, I was so closed off, I wasn't altogether sure how to have any kind of relationship.

Add in Brooks and Souta's preexisting relationship... If we wanted to make it work, we needed to let our relationships develop naturally. I knew these things, but they seemed to get buried under my fear of not being enough for them and wondering what my place was in their existing dynamic, what I needed to be.

Then twist in Michael, Ash, and Kelly, not to mention Souta's and JJ's families, and it became an overwhelming amount of people to connect with, to figure out where I fit.

The thought of even more people to connect with overwhelmed me.

The boys let me be for the first couple days, doing little more than making sure I ate and made it to class. The longer the fog lasted, though, the more worried they became. It was obvious in the way they hovered around me and their constant need to touch me. I wanted to reassure them, but I remained stuck in processing mode.

When trying to find my father, I never gave a single thought to the after, to what came next. I don't think I even truly registered I'd found him, and my search was complete, until I stood there in front of him.

School, Souta's, school, Souta's, the loop remained. Predictable actions, which made it easy to stay locked in my fog of thoughts: family, relationships, and back again.

By Thursday, the boys began having whispered conversations and shooting worried glances my way.

We loaded into Souta's car at the end of school on Friday, and I barely registered us driving in a different direction. After we stopped, I followed the boys in a daze around JJ's house to the studio. My butt found the bench I'd fallen asleep on the first time I came here. I pulled my feet up onto the bench, wrapped my arms around my knees and laid my head on them, my red hair falling into my face.

The bass thrummed, the drums beat, the voice wrapped around me.

My brain pounded. Too many questions. Too many worries. The pulse in my head conflicted with the music. Not enough information. Not enough time. Something was wrong. Wrong with the rhythm. Not the thoughts. The music. Not right. Not quite.

I shook my head, trying to get the tempo to work, to sound right. My eyes caught on black and red on the wall. Wrong. Wrong. I couldn't get it to mesh. Couldn't get the worry to stop or the questions to die.

Standing, my eyes fixed on the guitar. My hand reached out. Wrapped around the neck. Plucked it from the wall. Instinct took over. My hands moved slowly, picking out the tune. My eyes closed as the melody washed through my system. The pounding faded. The questions slowed. The worries eased.

My fingers sped up, found the tempo. I rocked to the music. Complete.

Breathing deeply for the first time in days, I tore into a chord, and my fingers flew over the strings. I barely noticed when the music around me slowed, then stopped. I lost myself in the music, playing until my fingers ached. I let the notes fade and kept my eyes closed until the only sound was the soft whispers of breath. The beat made sense now.

My eyes slid open to find the boys stock-still, jaws dropped. Blue, gold, and brown eyes wide, stared at me.

"Damn, hot stuff! That was awesome!" Souta spoke first, breaking the spell holding them.

JJ leaned into me, "Welcome back, firefly."

His breath whispered over my ear, lips so close he nearly kissed the tip as his black hair brushed against me. A large, familiar arm snaked around my waist to pull me into a slender chest. I inhaled deeply and leaned into the comfort he offered for a moment before pulling out of his embrace. I stepped back and turned, needing to put a little space between us and set the guitar into one of the nearby stands.

Grinning at my boys, I pushed back a strand of red hair that fell into my face. "Guess I've been a little out of it, huh?" I've run so hot and cold, I didn't know why the boys put up with me sometimes, and I couldn't figure out how to fix it.

Brooks closed the distance between us. He didn't say anything as his arms wrapped around me. His clean, fresh scent surrounded me, eased the tightness in my chest. From over Brooks' shoulder, I saw Souta grin and rush at me. He tore me out of Brooks' embrace and swung me around. I laughed and slapped his arms.

"Put me down!" Not that I was far off the floor.

When my feet found solid ground, I slid out from the circle of his arms.

My mind reminded me someone else might like to hear from me. "I should call Michael."

With nods all around, I was thankful the boys understood.

Things ended on weird notes the other day, but with my fog lifted, I found my curiosity piqued. Despite being completely out of my element, I kept wondering what it would feel like to have a family. To have a father, a brother, and a stepmother. To know something, anything, about my mother and who she'd been.

Sunlight warmed my face as I stepped outside for a bit of privacy. Pulling out my phone, I scrolled through the contacts, stopping for the briefest of moments on Ash's name. I didn't understand why Michael gave me his number. I didn't believe for one second that he would ever accept me. His reaction, while a bit extreme, didn't leave a lot of room for hope. I considered deleting it, but the idea I might need to call him in an emergency stopped me. I moved past it, finding Michael's number and hitting talk.

"Hello?" He answered after only a couple rings, sounding a bit distracted.

"Um. Hi. It's Seraphina." I stumbled over my

whole name at first, unused to using it but remembering I never asked him to use Sera.

"Seraphina! Hi. I'm so glad you called. I worried Ash's behavior might make you reluctant to contact me again, and I didn't get your number before you left." He sounded so genuine and caring. It warmed me inside, even as my stomach performed backflips.

Now that I was talking to him, I didn't know what to say.

"I, um, I just... I..." Tripping over my tongue wasn't the way to go, but I couldn't find words. My pounding heart didn't help matters.

A deep, rueful chuckle came across the line. "This is kind of awkward, isn't it? Look, I'm due at the station soon, but why don't we get some dinner Saturday? I can dig up some pictures of Calista."

I nodded before remembering he couldn't see me. "Yeah, that sounds good." A smile split my face, making my cheeks hurt. I wanted so much to know more, to know everything. "Can I call you while you're at work?"

I didn't know what the rules were for when he was at the station. How did that work anyway? Did firefighters work an eight-hour shift? I didn't think so. I swore I read something about them working for several days straight, but I couldn't be sure.

"It's better to text. I might not answer right away, but I will eventually answer, okay?"

"Okay."

"I have to go. Talk to you soon."

"Bye, um, Michael." I gnawed at my nails, unsure if I should call him dad or not.

"You don't have to, Seraphina, but I'd love it if you called me Dad."

I gulped as my stomach flip-flopped again. "Okay. Bye…D… Dad." The term felt odd tripping off my tongue, but I looked forward to getting used to it.

"Bye, Seraphina."

I hung up with a strange feeling settling inside me, like a hole I hadn't known existed was slowly filling up.

FOUR

Stepping back inside, I half expected to find myself buried under a pile of boys. Instead, I found them lounging. Bright gold curls fell across Brooks' forehead when he glanced up from the book propped up on the drum set.

"Hey, beautiful."

Souta tucked his phone back in his jeans pocket before smacking JJ's arm.

"Just a sec, man. Just… one more… almost…" As his whole arm moved over the page, gentle scratches of the pencil filled the dead space between his distracted words.

Not finished, but done for the moment he dropped the pencil, then pulled a thin sheet of paper from the back of the sketchbook and placed it over the drawing. He closed the book, setting it on the bench before he focused on me and stood.

Closing the distance between us, he cupped my face and ran his thumb over my lips. My stomach flipped at his touch.

"Firefly?" One perfect black brow rose in question over warm golden eyes.

"I'm okay. I promise." Mostly true, anyway. Eventually, I would be okay. There were a lot of things I still needed to work through. Stepping back, I snatched up the guitar I played earlier and shot him a grin. "Now what do you say we make some noise?"

The music helped wipe away the last of my fugue state. Ages passed since I'd last held a guitar, or it felt that way. May always managed to ensure I got to play, even after the accident with my guitar. We meshed beautifully from the first chord and played until JJ's mom invited us to dinner.

Being around JJ's family still wasn't entirely comfortable for me, which Souta seem to understand, so he made excuses for us, and we headed home.

Looking forward to a calm evening, my mind drifted as I studied Souta's profile as he drove. The boys and I never talked about what happened on my birthday. We became so focused on finding my father that everything else fell to the side. Catching glints of Souta's deep brown eyes as he drove, lots of questions and concerns about our relationship popped up, but I didn't let them out.

School the next day passed in an ordinary and boring fashion. Well, as boring as being an Elementum got, anyway. Unfortunately, uneventful meant there was nothing to stop me from musing back on recent events. And some of the questions I buried the day before resurfaced.

How did someone manage to be in one relationship, let alone three? They were all so different, what did they expect of me? Could I be what each of them needed me to be? What would happen if I couldn't? Would they turn away from me? What would that do to our Genus? And what was my place in that? They seemed so settled into the bond; where did I fit in? Could I manage to strengthen them? Or would being together be the thing that ripped them apart?

Nausea settled in my stomach as my head pounded. I couldn't stop the worries about our relationship and our Iunctura once they reared their ugly head. Worst-case scenarios kept popping into my head; plausible or not.

After school, when we got home, I complained of a migraine and headed straight to my room. For a second, after I closed the door, I considered locking it to ensure no one would bother me, but this wasn't my home. I didn't have a right to keep Souta or his folks out of rooms in their own home.

After about half an hour the house fell quiet. Antsy, I paced the small confines of the room. Needing to move more than a few steps to find my balance, and not wanting to bother anyone, I slipped out of the room.

In the entryway, I paused long enough to put my shoes on then dashed out and down the driveway.

At the street, I glanced in both directions to figure out which way to head. In the end, I decided it didn't matter, so I headed right.

Wind rushed at me, sending the short strands of my red hair flying. The gray, overcast sky and the heavy air indicated rain. I pulled up the hood of my jacket to help keep my hair in place, tucked my hands into my pockets, and let my easy stride carry me onward without much thought.

My entire body vibrated as I walked and bounced every few steps. I wanted to pull out the lighter I kept in my pocket and play, but I couldn't take a chance on someone seeing me.

I discovered the park a few minutes later. The green expanse stretched out, even with the hint of rain, people lounged around on the open grassy area. A large playground area contained happy kids and parents perched on benches, who looked relieved for the break. A small lake, or large pond, depending on your definition, reflected the gloomy sky. There were a couple brave men out on small rowboats, they must have rented from the boat shack nearby.

Wooden picnic tables sat under shade trees scattered throughout the park, ready to be used. The atmosphere seemed happy and peaceful, but too many people loitered around. Sitting near the lake might help. As I approached a bench near the water, a tiny dirt trail caught my eye.

Upon investigation, I discovered it to be a nature trail winding through a small copse of trees nearby. I couldn't tell where it led or where it would come out, but it looked like exactly what I needed.

The trail widened from a slim footpath to a real trail under the canopy of trees. Between the overcast, late afternoon sky and the shade of the tree branches, only minimal light made it onto the trail. I still itched to break out my lighter, especially since it would provide more illumination to ensure I didn't trip over my feet, but I didn't. I stretched out my hand, the tips of my fingers brushing against leaves and branches. Soft sounds of wildlife reached my ears. As I walked, allowing the natural serenity to wash over me, the tightness in my chest eased.

The trail turned sharply to reveal a high stone wall running along the right side of the trail. Every so often, an iron gate broke the white stone expanse. Shingled roofs and second stories rose from behind it, stretching to the sky. Vines peeked over the top of the wall, and some sections were already working their way down the wall on the woods' side. More light filtered through, not enough to truly brighten the trail, but I no longer felt immersed in gloom.

My head and heart mirrored the change on the trail. My thoughts came to a slow stop. The unsettling heaviness in my heart lifted. The boys cared about me. They wanted us to work, not just our Genus, but our relationships. I needed to remember that.

Maybe part of my panic came from all the recent changes in my life? Learning to adjust my thinking and feelings wasn't easy. Eighteen years didn't disappear in the blink of an eye because a couple guys decided they liked me. Or because I discovered one of my parents lived.

My stride shortened as the trail turned again. It snaked for a short distance, roots jutting up in an attempt to trip the unwary hiker. I started as gray-streaked across the path, chuckling when I spied the tiny rabbit twitching its nose in my general direction.

The path ran in a wide half-circle, eventually leading back to the lake.

I sank to the soft grass near the water, wrapping my arms around upraised knees. While my brain and heart seemed settled, a lot of questions remained unanswered. And maybe that was okay. I didn't need all the answers right now.

When pinks and oranges streaked across the surface of the water, I realized I'd been out longer than I thought. Rising, I ran a hand over my butt to rid myself of dirt and grass.

"Wooo, baby!" A deep male voice startled me. My head jerked up, swiveling to meet the waggling eyebrows of some human with a belly overflowing his jeans. "I'll rub that ass for you!"

I should let it go, but my temper flared. After Aguirre, I was determined to not be a victim.

I sauntered over, making sure to shake the ass he so badly wanted to rub. I batted my eyelashes, smiled coyly, and ran a finger over his chest. I leaned in, pressing my palm against him and heating it, not enough to hurt him but enough to be uncomfortable.

"Dream on," I murmured as his eyes widened, and I shoved hard.

He fell to his ass, hand rubbing the spot on his chest my hand just heated.

Turning on my heel, I left without another thought, making my way home to my boys.

———

Before stepping into the house, I took a deep breath. I wanted to talk to the guys. Before I could think about entering, the door flew open. Souta dashed out, screeching to a halt when he saw me standing there, dark eyes wide and wild, the slightly too long locks of his brown-black hair flying into his face.

"Sera!" He reached out, lifting me off my feet and spinning me around as he clutched me against his chest. "Where were you?" He set me on my feet again but hung on when I swayed.

"Nowhere important," I answered. "I need to talk to you. Are Brooks and JJ here?"

"Yeah, inside. Come on." Souta leaned in to peck my cheek before we walked back inside.

Brooks and JJ sat in the family room, concern on their faces.

"I'm sorry," I started after Souta curled up in Brooks' lap. "I shouldn't have snuck out."

Golden eyes watched me crossed the room as JJ shrugged. "We understand, firefly. At least, we think we do."

I wasn't so sure they did. "I needed time to think, by myself," I admitted. I perched on the edge of the couch, spine stiff, hands clutched tight between my knees. "Honestly? I realized we never talked about… what happened on my birthday or our Genus, or well, much of anything, actually, and my brain's starting to dredge up a lot of worries."

I expected their faces to fall, to see disappointment or anger, but only openness and concern crossed their faces.

"This has been a big change for me, and it's all happening at once. It's—" I stopped quickly as the realization hit me that I was babbling to ease the guilt churning my gut. "It's overwhelming."

Standing, I picked at my nails and started to pace. Would they hate me for wanting to figure things out? I couldn't seem to wait for things to happen on their own. My mind would latch on to the stray thoughts and worries, churning them up until they took over.

Brooks patted Souta's thigh, and he slid off him. He stood and crossed the room, wrapping his hands around mine to stop my fidgeting. I nearly pulled away but managed to stop myself at the last minute. Blue eyes like the ocean calmly gazed into mine, we stood still as he caressed my hands with his thumbs until I felt my nerves settle.

Souta patted the couch next to him. "C'mon, hot stuff. Sit down and talk to us." Gently I withdrew my hands from Brooks, shooting him a smile as I made my way to the couch and settled in. I drew my legs up, resting my arms on my knees, and breathed in deeply.

"You had some concerns, firefly?" JJ moved to sit on the floor in front of me, charcoal stained fingers grazing my bare foot.

I nodded. "Things happened so fast on my birthday and afterward, everything with Aguirre, me moving in with Souta, then we became hyper-focused on the search for my father." I stumbled to a halt, unsure what the point I wanted to make was, or how to say what I wanted to. Fingers grazed my foot again, another set running up my jean-clad calf.

"It's okay, beautiful. We're here. Whatever it is." Brooks' soft murmur in my ear washed over me, sending with it a shot of the confidence I needed so badly right then. I squeaked when Souta grabbed my hips, lifted me, and promptly deposited me on his lap. His fingers played in the short strands of my hair. I squirmed, the idea of sitting in a lap still a bit odd.

A light swat to my thigh stilled me. "Cut it out, hot stuff, please." Souta choked the words out, the compact muscles under me tensing. I almost smacked myself as his meaning sunk in. Shooting him a grin, I wiggled one more time. He swatted my thigh again, grunting, "Gonna kill me."

Gentle pressure on my foot sent shivers through me, "We want this to work." JJ brought my attention back to the matter at hand. "And talking about how we're feeling is going to be a big part of that, especially if we want to avoid Foederis."

"I'm worried about how you guys will feel. I know you talked about it and said jealousy wasn't an issue, but how can you be sure?" I shifted in Souta's lap to meet JJ's golden gaze better. My breath caught for a moment, still stunned by his good looks, "Especially you JJ. You've been the most, um, determined to date me. Now, I'll be dating you, but I'll also be spending time with Souta and Brooks. You and I won't be together as often because of that. Won't you be bothered by that?"

He reached up, grabbing my hand, and pressed

his lips to the back. "Firefly, why should it bother me? You'll come back to me, right back home, in my arms, where you belong. I know that. Even when you're with them, you're still mine, as much as you are theirs. I know when you're with me, I'll be your focus, and I know, beyond a shadow of a doubt, the four of us will make this work."

I wanted half the confidence his voice held.

"And I think we're a little past just dating, firefly. Nothing I feel for you is casual. As far I'm concerned, you're my girlfriend, and I'm pretty sure Brooks and Souta feel the same."

One of my worries eased as he easily defined our relationship. Hopefully, I could manage to live up to their expectations. A soft ding broke into the silence. JJ pulled his phone from his pocket, frowning as he checked it.

"I need to go. Sophie collapsed." The air seemed to get sucked out of the room with his words. "They're rushing her to the hospital."

"Want us to come with?" Brooks asked.

He shook his head, black hair waving with the motion, and shrugged. "No. Mom is freaking out right now, and we don't know what's going on."

He stood and tugged my hand, pulling me to my feet. Wrapping my arms around him, I squeezed tight, my pulse racing as I wondered what was going on with his sister.

He dropped a kiss on my forehead. "Keep talking. I'll call you later, and you can let me know what you talked about."

"Keep us updated," Souta called as he strode out.

JJ waved an acknowledgment as he caught Shiro's attention in the foyer and asked for a ride to the hospital. I wanted to chase after him, insist he let me come with him, but I wasn't family, so it wasn't my place, right? Instead, I tried to set my worry aside and focus on the rest of the conversation I needed to have.

Souta snagged my jeans and pulled me back into his lap. I couldn't help my eye roll. The way they kept tugging me around made me feel like a rag doll. But as tempting as it was to harass them for their behavior, this wasn't the time.

"I'll be honest, hot stuff." Souta ran his fingers up and down my arm. I fought against the desire to slide off his lap, wanting a little space, but I was learning that Souta tended to be tactile when things got serious. "I'm apparently a bit possessive, like I told you before. Right now, I'm fine with the idea. If that will hold true as we go forward? I don't know, but I won't let it hurt us."

I nodded, wondering if there was a story behind

discovering his possessiveness. I'd have to ask later. I swiveled to look at Brooks who'd taken a seat next to us on the couch. He smiled softly, blue eyes shining with fondness as they roamed over us.

"Your happiness is all I want." His finger slid down my cheek, then farther down between Souta and me. Gently, he tugged me off Souta's lap and into the space between them on the couch.

I blew out a breath, shooting him a grateful glance.

He leaned over, blond curls brushing against my cheeks and breath ghosting across my ear as he whispered, "Don't be afraid to tell us you're uncomfortable."

Needing a bit more space, I slid to the hardwood floor, laying down and tucking my hands behind my head. "This is another thing. How do we handle things with the three of us? I mean, you two already have an established relationship. Bringing me in is going to throw a monkey wrench into those works."

"Beautiful, how long, exactly, do you think Souta and I have been together?" Brooks rumbled softly.

I'd never thought about it. They seemed so settled in their relationship and all of them in their Genus, that I figured they'd been together for a while.

"I don't know. Five, six months at least?" I toyed with a loose gold thread on the couch.

Souta chuckled. "You are too cute, hot stuff." He shifted, laying his head in Brooks' lap and turning so he faced me. "We've only been together for about two months. Brooks moved to town just a couple weeks before my eighteenth birthday. JJ joined us about a month ago, but we've been friends for years."

Shock ran through me. Two months? And they'd only known each other for a couple weeks before they did what they did? Even still, I worried about being the third wheel. Would my relationship with each of them always come secondary to their relationship with each other? The knowledge of how short a time they'd been together led to another question. Dropping the thread, I traced the golden design against the deep crimson, debating exactly how to ask what I wanted to know.

"Um. I don't quite know how to ask this, but what about, um, physical stuff? You've been, well, active, right?" I cursed myself for stumbling over such a straightforward question. I'd never been shy, so why the hell was I tripping over my words? Red crawled up Brooks' neck and over his cheeks.

"No," he murmured.

No? But they'd said at Souta's they had? Huh?

"After what happened on my birthday, we decided to backtrack a bit." Souta rubbed his cheek against Brooks' jeans, one hand dropping over the side of the couch and grazing my stomach. "We hadn't known each other long, hot stuff. It was way too fast, and neither of us would have gotten physical in such a short time if Iunctura hadn't been driving us. We haven't been together like that since."

That was not the impression I'd gotten that first day, or heck, that first week. That day in the kitchen, he'd said he wouldn't have said anything to me if not for Iunctura. I thought it was because of how devoted he was to Brooks, had I been wrong?

"But the day we met?" I didn't know how to word the question. Thankfully, they caught on to my question.

"I'm still young, hot stuff. I'm horny as hell. Just because we agreed to slow the hell down doesn't mean I don't want to jump him all the fucking time." Souta poked his head over the side of the couch, gaze boring into mine. "Or you."

Was it hot in here or was it just me? My breath caught, and I squirmed.

"Besides, it felt… like something was missing," Brooks spoke up.

Souta nodded, then put his head back on Brooks' lap.

One incredibly horny boyfriend? Check.

Still confused? Also, check.

"And the day of our Iunctura, when you said you wouldn't have said anything—"

Souta exploded to his feet, hands on his hips and face as tight as his stance. "Because I wouldn't disrespect my best friend like that! And it wouldn't have been right without Brooks! I'm no cheater!"

As he stormed out of the room, I sat up slowly, trying to figure out what the heck just happened.

"What did I do?" I turned to Brooks, but his face mirrored my confusion.

"I don't know." Brooks' eyes came back to meet mine. "Implied he would cheat, somehow, I guess. He has a real issue with that."

Well, fuck. Had I just screwed up before we even got going?

Unsure what to say, we sat in silence.

Five minutes later, a calmer Souta returned slightly disheveled with his hair standing on end in places from being tugged on. He plopped down onto the couch before deliberately tipping over to smoosh his angular face back against Brooks' solid, jean-clad thigh.

"I'm sorry," he said to both of us. "Can we forget that happened, please?"

"Yeah," Brooks and I spoke in unison.

Brooks ran his fingers through Souta's silky hair, and I reached up to skate mine over his well-muscled arm.

After another moment of silence, Souta broke the tension. "I checked in with JJ. They found out Sophie is diabetic."

The abrupt subject change startled me, but the news sent my heart racing. I didn't know much about diabetes, and I couldn't imagine getting news like that. Cell phone in hand, I dialed JJ, needing to talk to him, to check on him.

A tap on my shoulder made me glance back at Souta. "Put it on speaker, hot stuff."

I nodded and hit the button as JJ picked up. "Hey, firefly."

Damn, he sounded rough. The desire to reach through the phone and hold him raced through me. "Souta told us." The words sounded flat and useless to me. Obviously, Souta told us, or we wouldn't be calling. "I don't—" Unable to find the words, I stopped abruptly.

"Is there anything we can do?" Brooks rumbled, hand resting on the back of my neck, thumb stroking.

I leaned into the comfort of his touch.

"We're just trying to wrap our heads around it, right now." Exhaustion laced JJ's voice. "And Mom is beating herself up for not noticing the signs."

"JJ, I—" Words failed me again as I tried to express my feelings.

"I know, firefly. I know." Even through his exhaustion, I heard the conviction of his words. "I need to go. I'll call you later, okay?"

"Yeah, okay." Hanging up never felt so hard before.

I just wanted to take away his worry and fear, but I didn't know how. Instead, I took comfort in Souta and Brooks, JJ never far from my thoughts or my heart.

FIVE

Two days later, I found myself sitting in a hole in the wall restaurant, my stomach churning, though I refused to show it. Despite its size, the inside was beautiful. Deep gray walls and slate flooring paired with light pine tables and chairs padded in the same deep gray to provide a sense of elegance. Large windows and a myriad of tiny sconces provided light and warmth. A waterfall feature in the front tinkled merrily. The place felt far too fancy to take your newly discovered daughter to. Would I even know anything on the menu?

At least I wasn't underdressed. Sitting across from me, Michael's broad frame, dressed in a dark-green, button-down and black slacks, drew more than one appreciative gaze. While I wore my black leather jacket and boots, I'd opted for a simple burgundy dress for dinner, one of the only outfits I owned appropriate for any kind of dressy event. Most of the others seated around us wore equally casual-dressy clothes.

"I know it feels fancy." Michael smiled as if he understood my discomfort. "But you'll love the food here, I hope. It's simple fare, well done and plentiful. And the best part?" Michael pointed to the front window.

I squinted to see what he was pointing at. In a corner of the window sat the compass symbol used by Elementum run establishments, symbolizing a safe zone.

No wonder the place was a hole in a wall. Truly safe places, ones where we didn't need to worry about our powers or watch what we said, were hard to establish in any city. The only way to truly keep it safe was to have a Sage hide it from human eyes. It made sense, though, to seek out an Elementum safe place for our first dinner. We wouldn't need to watch our words here.

"Hi!" a perky waitress in simple black pants and shirt greeted us. "I'm Marie. I'll be your waitress. What can I get you?"

Michael ordered coffee then tried to change my mind when I ordered water with lemon.

I shook my head. "I'm not big on coffee or sugary drinks, but thanks."

When the waitress left to get our drinks, I sighed quietly. Everything felt so awkward around him. Why did it have to be so hard to forge a relationship?

"Let's get this out of the way shall we?" Michael slid an envelope across the table. Stomach flipping, I picked it up, noting that someone opened it already. I knew what it was but not what it would say. "DNA results. You are most definitely my daughter."

My eyes scanned the words several times before they registered the truth of his statement. Right there in black-and-white, confirmation that the man in front of me was, in fact, my father. Would I be a good daughter for him? Did I know how to be a daughter? Butterflies turned into bullets in my stomach as I set the paper down.

"So, your mother," Michael broke the uncomfortable silence. "What did you want to know?"

"I don't know where to start." I unrolled my napkin, fiddling with the silverware. "I have more questions now than before."

Needing a moment, I looked over the menu,

pleased to find food I understood. The waitress came back with our drinks then took our order, giving me a few more minutes to figure things out. A light breeze brushed me as she floated the menus back toward the hostess station. Once she left, I didn't get a chance to ask anything.

"I should explain about Ash." Voice soft and low, Michael looked at the table, regret filling the brown eyes that matched my own.

"You don't have to," I said quickly.

Honestly, I just wanted to know more about my mother, right now, and how they'd met. Thinking about Ash and his rejection made nausea rise in my stomach.

"Actually, explaining Ash means telling you about your mom and me." Michael arranged his napkin and silverware as he spoke. The light from the sconces glinted off the silver. "I won't lie to you, and I don't want you to have any illusions. Some things may be hard to hear."

My hand fisted in the napkin, a hard knot forming in my stomach. While unsure what to expect or what I wanted to hear, I needed the truth. "I'm not fond of fiction." I lifted my head and met his eyes, not allowing my feelings to take over. "I don't need illusions, just the truth, no matter how hard."

Michael smiled fondly, his eyes shining but unfocused like he was lost in thought. "You've got steel in you, just like your mother."

The waitress interrupted, setting our plates down and bringing Michael back to the present. He nodded his thanks, then speared a bite of potato before continuing. "Your mother and I…" he paused long enough for me to shift uneasily in my chair. "We were never in love. Cali was an old friend from school, one of the few I stayed in touch with. She was a regular in my life, and she was there when I fell head over heels for Ash's mother, Krystal."

I liked knowing they'd had some kind of history, even if it had never been love between them. I'd never been a drama queen, and I wasn't going to start now by overreacting unnecessarily. Michael paused, eating a bit, and I suspect gathering his thoughts. One of the sconces flickered out at the next table, and a man in a waiter uniform strode over, pulling a lighter from his pocket and shooting a small flame to relight the sconce.

Michael spoke while I ate and listened. "It was a bit of a whirlwind romance, but we just fit seamlessly. Cali and Krystal became fast friends. Cali was even her maid of honor at our wedding. So, she knew how much I loved Ash's mother, Krystal, and how badly the accident that took her life shook me." His shoulders drooped, and his brown eyes unfocused as he appeared to get lost in memories.

Cautiously, I pressed my fingers against his in effort to draw him back. He startled, shook his head, then refocused on me. "Cali was always there, to comfort me or to help with Ash, who was so young at the time. We didn't plan for anything to happen between us. It just kind of did. It happened a few times, usually when things seemed darkest to me." I held back a shudder at the mental image trying to break through, of the two of them together. Ew.

"Then a couple months after the first time, she came by and told me she'd gotten an offer in North Carolina. I wanted her to be happy, to find the Genus she wanted so badly. So, I told her to go." Michael's smile fell from his face then, his shoulders slumped. "Now, I guess it was the wrong choice. I thought the move was the answer to her prayers. I'm so sorry."

The sheer amount of guilt emanating from him sank into me. Slowly, I reached across the table, placing my hand over his. "You had no way to know." I spoke with all the conviction I felt. "You did what you thought would make her happiest. That's pretty amazing." He'd thought of her desires before his own need to have a warm body and a helping hand. To me, that spoke volumes. He might not have been in love with my mother, but he cared about her.

He shook his head. "If I'd known…"

"But you didn't," I interrupted before he could continue down that road. "You made the best choice you could with the information you had. And we can't change it."

"We've lost so much time." He reached across the table to brush at my red hair.

I fought the instinctive urge to jerk back away from his touch. Reassuring him had been easy. Accepting his touch would be an uphill battle for me. Michael shook off his melancholy and smiled again.

"I'm sorry, got off track there." He picked up his coffee and grimaced when he sipped it before setting it down. "Cold."

Reaching across the table, I pressed my hand to the outside of the mug and heated it until steam curled from the top.

"Thanks." He sipped and sighed. "Much better."

"Now, I was explaining about Ash. After Cali left, I didn't think about what happened between us at all. Every time we spoke about Cali, it was as a friend and not a lover. But Krystal," he sighed, a wistful smile playing over his face. "I talked about her all the time. I loved her so much, and I wanted Ash to know everything about her, to love her as much as I did. She had no one, but us, to remember her. Without meaning to, my stories and memories built her up into a legend. It didn't help that I didn't date much after Krystal, either, not until Kelly. And she kind of barreled in and wouldn't leave. It took Ash a long time to come around to the idea of us."

I fiddled with my water glass, chasing stray droplets on the outside of the glass. "So, the other day was shock?"

"Likely." He shrugged.

I accepted it; after all, he couldn't exactly read Ash's mind. We might be capable of a lot of things, but not that.

"That doesn't excuse his behavior, though," Michael added. "He's not a bad guy, Seraphina. He'll come around."

I had my doubts, but for now, I'd keep them to myself. For the rest of the meal, Michael shared minor details about my mother, little things like stories from school and college.

"In college, we shared a small apartment with our friend Hugh." His grin lit up his brown eyes, and I found myself biting back one of my own, my stomach fluttered as I waited for him to continue. "He was a bit of a partier, and Cali was a light sleeper.

One semester, she had a class at seven in the morning, and Hugh would come stumbling in drunk at three in the morning, making enough noise to raise the dead. She finally had enough, and one night, she rigged an air horn to the front door. When he came home that night, it went off." His broad shoulders shook with laughter. "Not only did it wake both of us and scare him sober, but it woke up the gal across the hall and her three-month-old infant we didn't know about."

My eyes widened. Oh shit.

Michael laughed and nodded. "Yeah, after we got the lecture of a lifetime from an overtired new mom, we offered to make up for it by babysitting once a week for a month. She was all too happy to take us up on the offer."

The stories made her real to me for the first time.

"One Halloween, while Hugh and I were in class, she went around the apartment and put glow in the dark eye stickers on all the photos we had taped to walls. Neither of us noticed, not until we got up in the middle of the night and screamed because the possessed photos were watching us."

I almost fell out of my chair laughing. Apparently, my mother liked a good prank.

By the end of the evening, I felt more comfortable

around Michael, though I was still unsure how to be a daughter to him. I wished there was someone I could talk to, to find out if I was doing things right or not.

After he paid for our meal, Michael waited outside with me for the car Souta insisted I use, despite my protests.

A shiver ran through me. Though the air had cooled a bit as the sun set, it wasn't the reason for my reaction. I couldn't explain it. Something seemed off tonight, and for a moment, it almost felt like I was being watched.

I shook it off as a car pulled to the curb.

"Thank you for dinner." I turned to Michael. "I liked hearing about my mom."

"It was nice to remember." He smiled. "Why don't you come by the house in a couple days, get to know Kelly?"

"Sure." Souta honked, and I opened the passenger door, waving as I slid in.

As soon as Michael turned away and the door closed, a firm grip on my arm made me jump "How'd it go? Did it go well? It looked like it went well. He looks happy. You look, well… not happy, but not unhappy. Is he okay? Do you like him?"

My eyes widened at the sheer speed at which Souta whipped off questions.

"Oh my god." I laughed. "Take a breath."

Heat flashed in his brown eyes. He yanked me forward, hand reaching up to cup the back of my neck as our lips slammed together. I melted into him needing his familiar comfort. His tongue ran over my lips, and I parted them eagerly. Our tongues danced until I needed air.

Panting, I pulled back, swallowing hard at the way his heated gaze ran over me.

A shiver ran through me as he growled, "I missed you, hot stuff."

I raised a doubtful eyebrow. "I was only gone a couple hours."

"Way too long." Souta leaned in, drawing us close again, but I put my hand to his chest, stopping him.

"Drive. Before someone wonders what we're doing."

"Spoilsport," he muttered as he put the car in gear and took off. Flush from our kiss, I took a few deep breaths and tried to get my body back under control. As he drove us home, we talked about my dinner with Michael. His bubbly enthusiasm kept me laughing.

When we arrived home, he pulled me into the house. I stumbled on the green and black entry rug trying to keep up with him, waving at his parents as we passed them in the hall on the way to the second floor. I didn't bother asking Souta to slow down, he wouldn't, but it would have been nice to know why we were in such a hurry.

"Babe! We're home!" Souta called as he continued to tug me toward his room. He threw the door open, and seconds later, he pulled me down onto the bed with him. I sank into the soft blue comforter as he spooned me from behind.

"Cuddle time! Brooks, get your sexy ass over here." His arm came around my waist bringing us closer together and scooting us backward to make room. I'd failed to notice Brooks curled into an overstuffed blue armchair near the bed with a book in hand.

"Hello, sweethearts." Brooks grabbed a leather bookmark from the white side table, tucked it into his book, and set it down as he rose. He slipped into bed, maneuvering until he spooned me from the front. I laughed as the guys scooted in, nearly squishing me between them. It took a few minutes, but we eventually settled into comfortable positions, curled around each other.

"You seem surprisingly okay," Brooks whispered in my ear as his fingers stroked the soft cotton against my hip.

"She's better than okay. She's fuckin' fabulous."

Souta swatted at my rear as his lips left a peck on my neck.

"It was nice. I like him." I burrowed into the bed as I spoke.

I didn't want to move from here for the rest of the night. A hand stroked my side, sending shivers over me, while another stroked my hip. My eyes drifted closed under their gentle touches. Soft kisses pressed against my neck and collarbone. With a sigh, I took a moment to enjoy the intimacy. I liked being wrapped up in my boys, but my brain wouldn't let it go on for long.

A hand moved across my stomach, the fabric shifting until the fingers at my hip teased my bare skin. I stiffened when the fingers stroked over my thigh. They stilled, and I forced myself to relax. My mind refused to cooperate, though, overwhelmed by the physical contact, and I wiggled out from in between the guys.

"Sorry, just a little much touch right now." I tried to smile but failed.

Souta bounced off the bed, toe-walking over to me, and thankfully stopped without grabbing me, which was his usual move.

"It's okay, hot stuff. No big." He reached out and gently ran a finger down my cheek. "Why don't we watch a movie, and I'll ask Chris if he's up to fixing us a snack?"

If we watched a movie, we'd be in the family room where I could curl into one of the armchairs without hurting their feelings. Not to mention Chris, Souta's cook, made the best movie snacks. I nodded, and Souta grinned as he bounced out of the room.

Brooks rose from the bed. He ran a hand through his blond curls as if hoping to tame them.

"Come on, you two! What are we watching?" Souta's voice floated back to us.

Brooks chuckled, shaking his head as he leaned close. "We're not going anywhere, beautiful."

I knew that. In my heart, I knew.

My head, though, kept screaming loud enough to drown my heart out.

SIX

"C'mon, firefly, we don't want to be late."

JJ tugged my hand, drawing my attention back to him. I let him pull me along, but my gaze drifted back to where the Walrus, I mean Scholae, of the school stood talking to a guy who seriously gave me the creeps. I couldn't quite put a finger on why. There was just something about him.

He looked perfectly ordinary, one might say handsome, with short black hair, broad shoulders, average height and weight. Dressed in black jeans and a T-shirt, he could have been a local college guy. As if he felt my gaze on him, his head jerked around, and something unsettling glittered in his dark eyes.

A shudder ripped through me, and I closed the

small distance between JJ and me, squeezing his hand harder. My grip drew his attention.

"What's wrong?" He stopped, pulling me into his arms.

For once I didn't stiffen or pull away, needing his comfort at that moment.

"Who is that talking to Scholae Jones?"

JJ peered over me, then dropped a kiss on the top of my head before turning us to head into the school.

"Chester?"

Another shudder ran through me. "Who is he? He kind of creeps me out."

"I wouldn't worry too much about him. He's just the local whack job. He was a couple years ahead of Sandra, Brooks' sister, in school. According to her, he was obsessed with the Quintus myth. He's likely just bugging Jones about it."

I tried to put him out of my mind during the school day, but the creepy way his eyes were laser-focused on me kept returning. Something about him unsettled me, far more than JJ's brush off about him being a bit weird should.

And the Quintus myth? Why would he, or anyone, be so focused on that?

Determined to put the guy out of my mind, I flipped to a blank page in my notebook and tried to tune into Ms. Gallup. I liked Genus Studies, and now that I had one, the things I learned would be so much more important. Only a myth distracted me at the moment.

Supposedly, the Quintus was the fifth element, Spirit. No one really knew if they ever existed, though. The stories were few, far between, and vague. The ones the Tabularium possessed differed greatly in definitions of the powers of the Quintus, as well as their purpose. It wasn't like with my element or the boys. We could manipulate our element, a physical thing. Spirit wasn't a physical element, and none of the stories agreed on anything.

I listed the abilities I read about in the few stories online, some other facts from those stories, anything that I could remember. By the time class ended I developed quite a list, but still couldn't understand why that Chester guy would be so obsessed with the myth.

An arm wrapped around my waist; lips pressed against my neck while a hand gently tugged the notebook from my hands.

"Hot stuff, what is this?" Souta's lips moved against my neck as we duck walked down the hall.

I wriggled out of his grasp.

His eyes scanned the headings, brows drawing

together. "Quintus abilities? Why are you listing those?"

I shrugged. "Saw some guy talking to Jones this morning. JJ said he was obsessed with the Quintus myth. For some reason, I can't get my head to leave it alone, so I was trying to figure out why."

He shook his head and handed my notebook back. "If you can figure that one out, you'll solve the mystery of the century."

Brooks and JJ met us in the cafeteria, and as our talk turned to music, the mystery of Chester and the Quintus fell to the back of my mind.

When the boys' talk switched to other things, I pulled my phone out and flipped around, looking at random stuff, until something caught my attention.

"Hey, check this out. Did you guys know about this?" Unable to hide my flutter of excitement I turned my phone toward them, revealing the site I had up. They glanced at the screen, JJ leaned closer, while the other two shook their heads.

"Yeah, I think I've heard of this place. An old historical house; it's mainly a bunch of period stuff. Never been there."

"The site says they have old documents, diaries, newspapers, and stuff." The idea of being able to see and read old diaries thrilled me.

"Looks like exactly the kind of place you'd enjoy." Brooks leaned in to get a better look at the site as the bell rang.

Lunch never lasted long enough, dammit.

Tucking my phone back into my pocket, I grabbed my tray and tossed the remains of my lunch, then kissed Souta and Brooks before heading off to science with JJ.

Neither of us were doing well in Science, since we both tuned out Mr. Bearns's lectures. Thankfully, the experiments and lab work made up for our lack of book work.

Today, Bearns was in lecture mode, so JJ pulled out his sketchbook. I envied him the ability to look like he might be paying attention. Only, instead of taking notes, he sketched.

I rested my head on my hands and fought to keep my lids from closing.

When the bell rang, we both jumped, gathered our stuff, and followed the throng of people out the door.

We met Souta down the hall, and JJ passed me off with a quick kiss. I didn't miss the jealous glares around us.

Souta and I strolled into English hand-in-hand. We still got fleeting glances on occasion; sometimes it was confusion, but mostly it was people adjusting to the idea of Souta and me.

The bell rang as we sank into our chairs, and Mr. Rhinehart clapped his hands.

I leaned back and waited for him to impart whatever crap he'd spout today. For a young—and frankly good looking—man, he acted like a seventy-year-old stuffy English professor, complete with khaki pants and brown cardigan.

Although, I guess the professor part was true.

I didn't like English. The damn grammar rules had more exceptions than I could wrap my head around. Not to mention we read way too many fiction novels. I didn't mind learning about the people behind the stories, but the damn novels…

I'd rather shove an ice pick in my eye.

Okay, maybe not.

Still, I hated it.

A nudge to my foot yanked me out of my thoughts, and I glanced at Souta, who threw me a grin and nodded toward Mr. Rhinehart, who had started his regularly scheduled lecture mode while I got lost in my head.

"Shakespeare was, in my opinion, the greatest mind of his age. So, as we dive into his work I hope you develop an appreciation for the incredible works you read. We'll be doing a lot of in-class reading and discussion, but a major part of this unit will be a project done largely in your free time." He strode over to his desk and picked up a sheaf of papers. "I will be assigning you into groups or pairs and giving each of you a scene to work on from one of Shakespeare's iconic works. You'll have two weeks to prepare. You'll get assigned a date to present your project." He paced the front, his cardigan swishing.

Why did it swish that way? I'd never seen a cardigan do that. Was he a Ventus? I looked over at Souta, nudging his foot with mine to catch his attention.

When his gaze focused on me, I mouthed my question.

He nodded.

Well, that was one mystery solved.

"The project is broken into two parts: Performance and Discussion. For the performance part, you will need to memorize and perform a scene. For the discussion section, you'll talk about a different scene from the same play. The details of the play, the scenes, the talking points for the discussion are on these papers." Mr. Rhinehard held them up as if we hadn't been watching him pace with them. "A final note before I hand out assignments; the more effort you put in, the better your grade will be. While your assignment is nothing more than to memorize, perform, and talk about a specific piece, that is an average grade. You'll pass, but that's it. If you want to do better than average, you'll need to find creative ways to go beyond what's written on these sheets."

As he started handing out the assignments, I tuned him out and turned to Souta.

He raised an eyebrow. "What's up, hot stuff? You look like you have something on your mind?"

I shrugged a shoulder, but before I could say anything, Mr. Rhinehart's stuffy tone interrupted. "Ms. Embers. I don't believe this is the time or the place for whatever discussion you and your paramour were about to have."

Seriously? Paramour?

"You and Mr. Hicks will be working together on scenes from Romeo and Juliet."

"Dane?" Souta growled the name.

I glanced over at the guy who'd been seated on my right from day one and largely ignored. Mostly because I ended up focused on my boys instead.

A pale green eye winked at me as he took the papers from Mr. Rhinehart without looking. His blond hair, likely intended to look like some kind of messy bed head, stuck out at all angles like a porcupine. Combined with his wide grin, he was a reasonably attractive guy.

Judging by his wink, he knew it.

That last part made him less attractive, and thankfully, I didn't care at all.

"No way!" Souta's angry shout drew my attention back to him as he slammed his hands down on his desk. "She can't work with Dane!"

"I believe I'm the one who makes those decisions, Mr. Kurihara." Mr. Rhinehart speared him with a stern gaze, and Souta crossed his arms over his chest, scowl still firmly in place. "Now, you, Mr. Kurihara, will be working with Ms. Snow."

He tossed a packet of papers on Souta's desk and moved on.

"What's the matter, Sue?" Dane leered as he peered around me. "Worried I'll actually give your girl the attention she deserves? Can't be easy, after all, dividing your affection between two people."

As Souta growled, I grabbed his wrist, hoping my touch would soothe him the way I'd seen Brooks do many times. Souta took a couple deep breaths and appeared to calm down. But from the glare he shot at Dane, it was only surface deep.

I sighed, not sure how to diffuse the situation since I didn't understand what the problem was.

"Hey, Red," Dane said, catching my attention.

I glanced over at him with raised brows.

He shook the papers. "We're gonna have to work on this at your place. I'm in the dorms during the week. Not a chance of getting shit done."

"First, don't call me Red, my name is Sera." I ran my thumb along Souta's pulse point, my next words might not thrill the hell out of him. "I guess we can work on this at my place, or rather Souta's place, since that's where I live. I don't think his parents will mind."

It was only a school project, not a big deal.

But the scowl didn't leave Souta's face for the rest of class, and I only caught half of the lecture because I kept trying to do what I could to help calm him.

Nothing worked, though.

When the bell rang, I twined myself around Souta and headed out.

A hand stopped me as we reached the door.

Dane held his phone out. "I need your digits, Red."

Shooting him a glare, I typed in my number and slapped the phone into his waiting palm. "Sera. S-E-R-A. Try to remember it."

The fucker winked at me again and walked off.

The farther away Dane got, the more Souta relaxed as we headed toward the gym.

Then, my phone went off.

And I made the mistake of checking it, with Souta right there, able to read every word.

Dane: Hey, Red. What time will I be cuming?

Souta growled, I sighed and texted Dane back.

Sera: Really? Go fuck yourself. We'll discuss the project tomorrow. In class.

What the fuck was this guy up to?

"He's not allowed in my house, Sera." The vehemence in Souta's voice surprised me.

He'd turned to face me, lips pressed white, arms crossed over his chest, stiff as a board. I decided not to let Dane come to Souta's place after all, given Dane's apparent need to irritate him, but Souta didn't know that.

"He isn't coming to the house and, certainly, not tonight. I'll figure something out on how to work with the guy. Not like I have much choice."

"You didn't exactly put up a fight!" Souta's voice rose, turning heads toward us.

I didn't know what to do or how to handle his anger. I wished Brooks were here. He always calmed him down, but despite discreetly peering around, I didn't see him.

"You know what? Forget it." Souta turned and stormed off to the locker room.

Wonderful. Less than a month into a relationship, and I was already fucking things up.

Ignoring the others in the locker room, I tossed my bag into my locker and dug out my clothes. P.E. remained my least favorite class and now that we were getting into some hard-core powers training, it really sucked. At least two people were guaranteed to end up needing a nurse before the end of the period.

I hoped Brooks had been able to calm Souta down.

Two steps into the gym I knew my hopes were in vain. Souta stood stiffly off to the side of the bleachers everyone else sat on, waiting for class to start. I trudged over and plopped down next to Brooks.

He curled his arm around me, pulling me into his side.

JJ sat next to me and pulled my feet up into his lap. "He's still pissed?"

"Yeah, What happened?" Brooks asked.

I guess Souta didn't tell Brooks anything.

"I got partnered with Dane Hicks for some English project, and Souta kind of lost his mind." Okay, slight exaggeration, but seriously, only slight.

"Dane Hicks?" JJ straightened up. "No wonder he

lost it. That guy is infamous for being a crass jackass who pretty much just wants into the pants of anything with boobs. Every time he's partnered with a girl, they almost immediately start sleeping together, really obviously. Then, the second the project is over, he dumps the girl."

"Hey, JJ."

I glanced up and nearly copied Souta's growl from earlier. A pretty brunette not-so-casually leaned toward JJ. She needed a little less cleavage considering this was PE. She also needed to stop showing her assets to JJ.

"Hey, Britt." JJ didn't even look up. "Anyway, like I was saying. Dane Hicks is bad news when it comes to being partnered with girls. He's broken up several couples. So far, he hasn't caused a Foederis—breaking a bond isn't exactly easy, after all—but I wouldn't be at all surprised if he did before the end of the year."

"He doesn't need to be anywhere near our girl," Brooks spoke up, meeting JJ's eyes over my head.

"Agreed. Not much we can do about it, though." JJ shrugged.

Angry at being talked over, I sat up, dropped my feet abruptly to the floor, and stood in one motion. "Or you could trust me not to fall for his shit!"

Heat moved through me, and I clenched a fist at my side as I stormed away.

What the fucking hell? I got it. The guy was a dick of the first order and enjoyed being one, but did they really think I'd fall for some asshole's quick moves?

"Alright, you guys, pair off, and let's get to it."

No one moved since the Coach's words were misleading. He would pair us off how he wanted.

As he ran over the bleachers and started pairing people off, I paced, needing to move from all the energy cooped up inside me.

Coach called my name, "Sera, work with Souta. Britt, work with JJ. Brooks, work with Vera…"

I tuned out as he moved on, waiting for Souta to join me.

We found a spot on the floor, far enough from the others that hopefully we wouldn't end up with any collateral damage. Neither of us spoke as we faced each other. We just stared at each other. For way too long.

Long enough that we caught Coach's attention. "Sera, Souta! Get to it!"

Souta thrust out a hand, a blast of wind flowing forward.

I should dodge it, that was the point of the

training after all, but I just let it flow around me. He didn't have enough power to knock me down; that kind of power only came with tons of training and experience. I pulled my lighter out of my pocket, a simple disposable that could be picked up for a dollar at any gas station, and flicked it. With my other hand, I pulled the tiny flame from the lighter then tucked it back into my pocket. The flame flickered softly on my hand as I moved my fingers, working the flame bigger.

"You need to ask for a new partner!" Souta's voice broke my concentration, and the flame shrank back down.

When I glanced up, he'd moved closer. Now, a mere two feet separated us as opposed to the six feet we were supposed to keep between us.

Heat flared through me that had nothing to do with the flame I held. My free hand fisted at my side, my jaw clenching as I took a couple steps closer. I was done with this. "You need to trust me!"

Why the hell was he making such a big deal of this? Where the hell did my happy, easy-going, excitable guy go? I shook my hand until the flame flickered out. If he planned to continue harassing me, I was leaving. Fuck the grade. I'd talk to him again when he had time to cool down.

"You know what? I'm done with this jealousy shit." I turned on my heel and headed for the exit.

However, I didn't get very far. A hand clamped down on my forearm and spun me back around.

"Don't walk away, dammit! You don't know him!" Souta got in my face, and my blood boiled. "Why won't you listen to me?"

Pure anger flashed through me as my hands found his chest, and I shoved him. "Let me g—"

His shocked yell cut off my words, drawing the attention of everyone not already watching us, including Coach. All the heat and anger drained from my body as I stared at the perfect smoking handprint burned through Souta's shirt, the exposed skin bright-red and beginning to blister.

What the fuck had I done?

"Souta!"

He swayed, and I lunged forward, arms wrapping around him, careful to avoid touching the fresh burns.

Coach spoke softly into the sudden silence, "Sera, get him to the nurse."

Tears burned in my eyes, and thankful for the calm direction, I nodded. With my arm around Souta, we headed out of the gym and toward the nurse.

The fight of moments ago shrank to minuscule proportions, and my stomach rolled. Look where my anger got me. "I'll talk to Mr. Rhinehart tomorrow." A tear slipped down my cheek, but Souta remained silent, from pain or irritation, I didn't know.

When we stepped through the glass doors to the front office, Ms. Jones glanced up and waved us on to the nurse. Of all the adults in this school, Ms. Jones was by far my favorite. As a Menda, she had no powers, despite both her parents being Elementum. A lot of people looked down on them, thought of them as inferior. Slung the nasty slur, Impar, at them.

I had nothing but sympathy for them. I knew what being an outsider felt like, and I could only imagine how hard it was to know our world existed, to grow up around all the myth, lore, and magic, and be unable to be truly a part of it.

Ms. Jones was sweet but made of steel. She didn't let anyone get away with anything and seemed to practically keep this Illustratio Conservatory running single-handed.

Nurse Holland waited at the entrance to the clinic, face impassive. "Coach called and let me know you were coming."

We headed in, and Souta hopped up on the table-bed-thing as Nurse Holland washed her hands and pulled on gloves.

I didn't want to see Souta in pain. Pain I put him in. Outside the room, I sunk into a nearby chair and let myself fall into my thoughts.

A few minutes later, Souta emerged sporting a new black and red striped shirt over his bandaged chest, and we left.

SEVEN

L ater that afternoon, back at Souta's house, with the stuff that happened at school still running through my head, restlessness took over. I found myself unable to stay still. The walls were closing in on me, and I needed to get out, to move, to let my mind drift and hope to clear it out.

"You okay?" Souta frowned as he rose from the blue armchair. His fingers wrapped around mine, halting the pacing I'd begun without realizing.

My gaze darted around Souta's room. Several large pillows in blue- and tan- striped cases leaned against the clean lines of the dark wood headboard. A matching dresser next to it held a black bowl with Souta's wallet and keys. A blue overstuffed armchair sat in a corner next to a white side table where a black metal lamp with frosted glass shade provided light. Across from the closet, most of the wall was taken up by a corkboard framed in black, featuring photos tacked up next to posters of dancers I didn't recognize. A round, blue and tan area rug took up most of the remaining floor space. The most notable things in the room, though, were the three concerned faces.

"I don't..." Not knowing how to answer I stalled.

Was I okay? Unable to keep my mind focused, I honestly wasn't sure.

Brooks rose, unfolding his long, jean-clad legs from the armchair he'd curled into. My attention caught on him as he crossed the room, the innate grace combined with those blond curls and piercing blue eyes making my brain stutter to a stop for a moment.

His hand reached out, a long, slender finger stroking my cheek then lifting my chin to meet his eyes. "Go for a walk. Take your phone, just in case, and come back to us soon." He punctuated his soft words with a gentle kiss to the corner of my mouth.

Drawing back, he twined his fingers around Souta's, releasing his hand from mine to wrapping his arms around Souta's waist.

As I left, I caught Brooks' words to Souta. "Let

her go. She needs a little time to herself. Our girl will be back."

I didn't know what I did to deserve him, any of them really, but especially Brooks with his amazing ability to understand what I needed.

My feet followed the same path I'd taken the last time I found myself needing time to think. Shying away from my relationship with the guys and how I burned Souta during class, my mind turned instead to my recently discovered family.

I had been back to Michael's getting to know him and Kelly better. My future stepmother's sweet and accepting nature put me at ease, and we discovered a shared love of history.

Despite my fears, I was starting to relax around them.

I wished I could get to know Ash, though. Michael kept assuring me he would come around, but the memory of his hateful glare sent a shudder ripping through me, a chill raising goosebumps on my arms. I glanced around, but only trees and the walls behind the homes surrounded me. Giving myself a shake, I realized it's stupid of me to let a memory affect me so much.

Which let my head find its way to the real reason I needed a moment away from the guys, the events from training this afternoon. How did the power flare happen? I sure as heck wasn't powerful enough to cause blistering burns or sear away a cotton tee in an instant. I had never done more than make a person uncomfortable with my heating ability, so how the fuck had I burned Souta so bad?

It shouldn't be possible, but I had burned him. More worrying to me was, would it happen again? How the fuck did I keep it from happening? Did I dare touch the boys when I didn't know how the hell I burned Souta?

My stomach cramped at the thought of causing the same burns on JJ or Brooks, or worse. They wouldn't let me not touch them, though. With too many questions and not enough answers, I kicked leaves from my path and debated what I should do.

Something hard crashed into me and sent me sprawling to my ass. Shoving my hair out of my eyes, I spied another form sprawled on the ground opposite me. All I could see was a pair of thin, jean-clad legs until the person sat up enough to look back at me. Brilliant blue eyes thickly lined met my own, amusement sparkling in them.

"Sorry."

"Sorry."

We spoke at the same time.

We stood, and I couldn't help but laugh as I brushed dirt and leaves off myself, all my previous thoughts scattered. "I'm really sorry. My head wasn't here."

The surprisingly small guy in front of me stood a good half a head shorter than my average height. Black hair fell across his forehead and into one eye. A tattoo of wind, or maybe waves, wrapped around one forearm and disappeared into the rolled-up sleeve of his black button-down.

"Mine, either." Something in the way he spoke those two words, in the way his face fell, and his eyes fixed on the ground, spoke volumes.

"You okay?" Seriously, this guy looked like he needed a friend.

Maybe talking to him would give me a break from my thoughts and help me figure out the whole power flare mess.

His eyes lifted, and he shot me a small smile. "Oh, physically I'll be fine."

He swiped a hand through the air, dismissing our run-in, and the light caught on several silver bangles around his wrist. As he skirted around me, I couldn't dismiss the pure pain radiating off him.

I spun and flung out my arm to catch his, then dropped it quickly before we reached the awkward, uncomfortable stage. "I'm sorry. Are you sure you're alright? You just don't seem like it."

He turned back to me. "It's got nothing to do with our run-in. My heart hurts, and that's not on you."

I knew about hurting hearts. "I get that."

No doubt our hurts were very different, but still, I found it easy to empathize as I tucked my hands into jean pockets.

"You, too, huh?"

I nodded.

We stood in a not-quite-awkward, not-quite-comfortable silence, caught in some sort of mutual empathetic spell.

"Skyler." Breaking the spell, he thrust out a hand.

I shook it. "Sera."

He jerked his head to the side of the path. "Wanna sit?"

Part of me said no, my reluctance to connect with others still strong, but another part wanted to make a connection. I shook off my hesitation and nodded.

We found a shaded spot to sit.

Skyler's bangles clinked as he rested his arms on his up drawn legs. "So, I just had a four-year relationship end. You?"

Wow. He was quite open with a stranger.

Although, what did he really tell me? Was this how these sorts of things went?

With nothing to lose, I jumped in with both feet. "I hurt my boyfriend without meaning to."

I picked at my cuticles, mind reliving this afternoon's events.

"Whoa, you wanna talk about it?" He shoved his hair out of his face, and I noticed his dark-blue eyes were lined in purple and multi-colored crystals sparkled on his ears.

I shook my head. "Not really." I didn't think I would be able to explain without going into details a human shouldn't know, like how I controlled fire or heated my hands up. "You?"

Skylar shook his head, pitch-black hair falling back across his face.

Silence fell, slightly awkward though not as much as it should have been.

Laughter broke the silence, and we watched as two young boys ran down the path. One held his hand out as though to tag the other, their appearance similar enough to be related.

Skylar grinned as they rounded the path out of our sight. "Look like brothers." Leaning back on his hands, Skylar turned his face toward me. "You have any siblings?"

I couldn't talk about my issues with Souta without revealing my abilities, but my issues with Ash were another matter. Could an outsider's perspective help?

Drawing my knees up, I rested my arms on them. "I actually just found out I have a half-brother."

"That's— What's that like?"

"Weird." Long strands of grass waved in the cool breeze, and I ran my fingers over them, letting them tickle my palm. "I'm not sure he likes me. His reaction when he found out was extreme."

"Shock will do that. It's likely, once he calms down, he'll at least be civil."

"My father keeps telling me something similar. It's hard to believe, though."

"Chances are good your father's right. I'm assuming the father is his as well?" At his question, I nodded, and he continued, sitting back up as he spoke. "It might not be easy but try to trust him. At least your father's accepting you. Not everyone is so lucky."

His face fell at his heavy words. I didn't know what to say or how to ask about the statement. I wasn't sure I really should, but a desire to offer comfort raced through me, and I reached over, gently laying my fingers over the top of his for a moment.

Skyler stared at our hands. "When I told my parents I was gay, they threw me out. I don't have any siblings, and my boyfriend was all I had. I moved in with him."

My heart hurt for him, to be rejected like that. I couldn't imagine the pain. "I'm sorry." It seemed feeble, but it was all I could think to say.

Skylar shrugged. "It was years ago. I have a few close friends I consider family now." Shaking the hair out of his face, Skylar grinned wide and waved a hand through the air. The breeze picked up for a moment, blowing my neon-red strands around to whip at my cheeks. "I didn't mean to get so serious. Tell me, ever heard of The Scribblers?"

With the mention of my favorite indie band, our talk turned to more superficial things, and we discovered a shared love of indie music, me for playing and him for listening.

We were discussing the lyrics of "Moonlighting" when Skylar looked up. Only then did I notice the lengthening shadows. The clicking of Skyler's bangles drew my attention as he checked a slender watch. "I should go. I'm due to meet some friends at a bar."

I grinned. Who wore a watch anymore?

Then his words registered, and my eyebrows

raised. "Bar? Um… How old are you?" I cringed internally at how rude I sounded.

Thankfully, Skyler laughed. "I get that a lot. I'm twenty-five."

He rose, brushed dirt off his jeans, and held a handout.

I accepted the help up.

As soon as I found my feet, he released me and turned to head off. "Maybe, I'll see you around."

"Maybe," I replied with a smile, feeling like I made a potential friend.

With a wave, he walked down the path.

I continued the opposite way down the path and tried not to let my mind settle back on my earlier questions about my power fluctuations. Answers weren't likely to come with the same worries and fears going round-and-round in my head. The whys of those fluctuations and the answers to my fears needed information I didn't have. I doubted I'd find the answers I needed in the online archives, though I'd check there first. Likely, I needed a trip to the Tabularium or a phone call to May.

As for what happened with Souta? My feelings on the matter were wrapped up with my guilt. Time to stop hiding from the boys.

When I reached the house, my hands shook at the thought of talking to Souta.

I wanted to head up to my room, close the door, and ignore the whole thing until we both forgot what happened. Not the healthiest way to handle things. Or at least, I didn't think so. Since I'd never been forced to deal with something like this, I wasn't entirely sure. I did know I wanted Souta and me to be okay.

Figuring the boys were still watching the movie, I walked inside and headed to the den, where I paused in the doorway to peek in.

An action movie was playing on the TV. Brooks sat against one side of the couch, one leg on the floor while the other rested on the couch. His arms loosely held Souta, curled against him, face buried in Brooks' chest, hands fisted in his red shirt. I wanted to go over there, wrap my arms around him, too, but didn't know if I'd be welcome.

"Get over here, beautiful." Brooks' voice barely reached me as his hand rubbed circles on Souta's back.

Was something wrong? Did I do more damage than we thought when I burned Souta? Was he mad at me? Why was he curled into Brooks like his world ended?

I tried not to let my face show my thoughts, but I failed as Brooks said, "He's fine. Just needing a little calming snuggle."

Slowly, my steps brought me across the hardwood floor within touching range, but I hesitated. "Is it my fault?"

Of all the questions in my head, that was the most prevalent.

"Sit." Brooks reached around Souta and patted the couch next to him.

My hand found my fingers and began picking at the cuticle as I sank onto the couch. I didn't know what to say or how to make things right, and Brooks didn't answer my question, so I could only assume Souta was upset with me.

"I'm sorry, Souta." My voice cracked as my eyes fixed to the floor. "I don't know what happened. I didn't mean to do anything. I didn't mean to use any power at all."

A hand wrapped itself around mine, stilling my fidgeting. "I hate when you do that, hot stuff."

My gaze jerked up. Souta had uncurled.

I took him in, but he looked okay. He looked great in fact. No red eyes or tear streaks. Chest bare, the burns covered with large gauze patches. My pulse sped up, breath catching in my throat as I took in his muscled chest.

Forcing my gaze off his body, I turned my hand, lacing our fingers together. Relief flooded through me when he didn't pull away.

"I know it was an accident." Souta slid closer, the dark pools of his eyes holding me captive. "And I think I have more to apologize for than you. My jealousy got the better of me today. It's just…" Souta blew out a breath and ran his hand through his brown-black hair. "I know Dane. He's got a reputation. When he sets his sights on a girl, he always gets what he wants."

"Mr. Rhinehart isn't known for being the most cooperative or understanding person, but if you're asking me to, I can request a new partner." Somehow, I didn't think *my boyfriend doesn't like my partner* would fly as a reason for needing a new one.

"No. That will never work. Besides, I need to get over this and trust in you." Souta untangled our hands and opened his arms.

I only hesitated for a second before I leaned in and hugged him. From the tight squeeze he gave me, he wanted to hang on longer, so I shifted to lean against him, careful to avoid the bandaged burns.

"I think I made a friend today." Considering how

Souta reacted to Dane, I didn't want to hide my meeting with Skylar and upset him further.

"On your walk?" Souta's fingers caressed my arm, sending shivers through me, little jolts of pleasure straight to my core.

Doing my best to hide my reaction, I nodded. "Literally ran into him, and we ended up talking a bit, mostly about trivial things."

"Thank you for telling me, hot stuff." Lips pressed against my hair, and we turned our attention to the movie.

"Valentine's day is coming up," Brooks said softly a short time later as his arm wrapped around both Souta and me. I struggled with why it mattered for a full minute until it hit me. For the first time ever, I was in a relationship, and Valentine's Day was supposed to be special for couples. Well, fuck. How the heck did I handle that with three guys? What was I supposed to do?

Souta nodded. "JJ and I were talking about that. None of us has had a chance to take you out yet. Would you be okay if we all wanted to do something with you individually, hot stuff?"

Since I didn't have any preconceived notions about Valentine's Day, I nodded. "But can we not do the dates all on the same day?" I spoke as the thought occurred to me. "I'd like to be able to spend as much time as we want together."

Souta and Brooks agreed, and when I texted JJ, he thought it was a great idea. Feeling calmer, I settled in to finish the movie with the boys, looking forward to my dates.

EIGHT

"Where are we going?" I asked Souta, peering at him and trying to read his expression.

Since the grin he wore was a perpetual thing, it told me nothing. His dark eyes lit with mischievousness as he pulled me into him and pressed a firm kiss against my lips.

"No questions allowed, hot stuff." Despite the teasing tone, there could be no mistaking the steel of his words, the command in his voice never failing to send a shot of pure desire through me.

He grabbed my hand, tugging me along to the sleek, black sedan he preferred when he drove. I opened my mouth to repeat my question, but he kissed me again as he opened the door, tucking me into the car with a waggle of his brows.

I couldn't stop wondering and worrying a little about what he had in mind. We'd been curled up together, watching a movie in his room, when he'd jumped up and told me it was time for our date. In a pair of torn black jeans and black mesh shirt, my biggest concern wasn't being dressed right since Souta wore a pair of fitted dark-wash jeans, a long-sleeved, turquoise button-down and a lightweight black jacket.

I waited for Souta to climb into the driver's side, but instead, he reopened the door. "Be right back. Forgot something."

What on earth? Maybe one of the others could shed some light on what was happening.

Sera: Souta is taking me out and being mysterious. Someone tell me what's going on?

I waited anxiously for a response. Surprises weren't something I dealt with well, but I'd never bothered to tell the guys. It never occurred to me I needed to tell them.

JJ: I'm told you've been instructed to not ask questions.

I frowned at my phone. He'd asked Souta?

Sera: You weren't supposed to tell!

JJ: Behave, firefly. Souta likes his surprises, and they almost always turn out well.

My brows rose nearly to my hairline.

Sera: Almost?!!?

JJ: It will be fine. Sit back and enjoy the ride. Talk to you later.

I glanced up in time to spy Souta bounce-walk his way back to the car. A large, old fashion style, white wicker basket hung from one arm, and a black and green plaid blanket draped over his shoulder. My leather jacket dangled from the fingers of one hand. He opened the door to the back, sliding the basket, blanket, and jacket in before closing it and making his way around to the driver's side.

"I thought you might need the jacket since your shirt is kind of thin, even with the tank under it." He turned the car on, and we were off without another hint to our destination.

I picked at my cuticles, dying for answers.

At the first stoplight, Souta leaned toward me. "Don't think I don't know about you asking JJ what's going on. I might have to spank you later."

The husky tone of his voice caused me to shiver. The idea of being spanked caused apprehension to war with anticipation. I knew about spanking; I was a teenager with internet access after all. Though he flirted a lot, he tended toward more aggressive advances with me since our Iunctura, and I couldn't tell how serious they were. I needed to trust that he wouldn't push things.

The drive was too short for my worry to fully take over and affect my mood. We pulled into a lot near a park with plenty of other cars. As I got out, I noticed it was the same park where I'd gone on my walk. We could have walked here, though it was a bit of a distance.

Maybe Souta planned something after this?

He grabbed the stuff from the back, then took my hand. When we hit the main entrance to the park area, my eyes widened at the number of people milling around. Overcast skies blocked any hope of the sun warming the cool air around us. I slipped my jacket on, grateful Souta thought to bring it along.

"What's going on?" I moved closer to Souta out of necessity as we made our way through the crowd.

As he guided me through the throng of people scattered around the lush, green grass and around a copse of barren trees, I spied white tent tops scattered around the lake. Off to one side, a stage set with scaffolding and lights stood ready for performers.

I froze.

"Keep moving, hot stuff." Souta's voice shook

with laughter. "We need to find a good spot before they start." Stumbling forward when he pressed against my back, I caught myself and headed toward the field where others already spread out blankets or put up lawn chairs.

My pulse sped up as I eyeballed the stage. Part of me wanted to be up there, singing my heart out, chords filling the air from my guitar, the energy from the audience feeding the atmosphere. Oh, who was I kidding? All of me wanted to be up there!

We found a spot close enough to have a good view but far enough to save our hearing and have a space for ourselves.

We spread out the blanket. While I worried about getting the soft, colorful piece dirty, Souta didn't show any hesitation. He plopped the basket down, pulling four small weights out of it and using them hold the corners of the blanket down. I couldn't help the grin that escaped me. Most people might think him flighty, but he was always prepared, always thought things through.

Sinking down, I watched him unpack the food. As plastic container after plastic container appeared, my stomach growled. Souta looked up, catching my eye, a smile fighting to free itself. Laughter escaped, freeing my own.

"I guess I'm kind of hungry." I grabbed one of the containers, half expecting to have it taken away.

"Obviously." Souta laughed, pulling a package of hand wipes out of the basket and tossing them onto the blanket. "You've barely eaten today." He met my gaze, dark eyes going serious, and laughter faded from his voice. "That's not like you."

I shrugged. "I guess I didn't think about it."

It happened sometimes, on a rare, lazy day.

Souta's usual fidgeting stilled, brows drawing together.

I leaned forward, my thumb smoothing his brow. "Honestly. I didn't realize I hadn't eaten. There's nothing wrong. I promise." I smiled, shifting to set the container I held down. "My emotions don't affect my appetite. But I don't always realize I haven't eaten when it's an easy, casual day unless my stomach screams at me."

I shrugged, hoping I'd conveyed it well enough for him to understand and to help his concern. It didn't happen often.

"As long as you're sure." He squeezed my hand before releasing it.

I popped open the container next to me to find a variety of cut fruit. Snagging a cut strawberry, I savored its sweet, tart flavor. The other containers opened to reveal chicken and egg salad sandwiches, veggies with dip, and my favorite cinnamon chip cookies.

Grinning, I grabbed a cookie and downed half of it in one bite.

It didn't escape my notice Souta brought only finger foods. Despite Souta's outward nature, he possessed a practical streak he tried to keep under wraps.

A guitar cut through the air, notes I knew by heart, could play without thinking about it. I whipped my head back to the stage, pulse speeding up as the hot-pink-haired lead belted out lyrics in her familiar, throaty voice. I wanted to squeal. Once I discovered them, The Scribblers became my favorite local indie band.

Practically vibrating with happiness, I twisted and threw my arms around Souta, lounging on the blanket next to me. "How did you know they were playing?"

He grinned, giving me a quick squeeze and kiss, as the wind suddenly picked up and swirled around us. He kept his arms wrapped around me. "I didn't. I knew about this free outdoor indie fest thing, and you've been listening to a lot of the local indie bands, but they don't advertise who's playing. I took a chance."

Since he didn't seem in any hurry to let me go, I settled in against him, picking at the food as I let my favorite songs wash over me.

After a couple songs, movement caught my eye. Glancing down, I spotted the fruit slowly jumping around in its container and dancing around in circles in time to the music. I tried to hold in a giggle.

Souta leaned down, his warm breath flowing across my ear and sending a shiver through me. "Watch this."

The fruit separated into types, each creating its own ring, moving independently. The individual fruits rose, just above the container's edge, and fell in patterns too quick for me to catch entirely, but the whole thing moved to the beat of the music. I glanced around, nervous since he decided to play in a public area, but everyone was tuned in to the stage.

I dug my fingers into his side. "Cut it out before someone sees."

The fruit marched its way once more around the container as he chuckled. The fingers controlling the fruit a moment ago skimmed over my belly. I arched into the light touch, tiny darts of pleasure shooting through me. Grabbing his wandering hand, I laced our fingers together and turned my attention back to the stage. We let ourselves get lost in the music.

A couple songs later, a familiar head of pitch-black hair caught my eye. Skylar's dark-blue gaze collided with mine, and he grinned. The emerging sun warmed us enough to be comfortable despite the cool temperature and glinted off Skylar's silver bangles when he waved.

He strolled toward us, hips swaying in the skintight black jeans he wore. His dark hair fell into his eyes when he nodded at us. "Hey, Sera. I thought I would see you here today. This the boyfriend?" He held a handout, and I noticed he'd painted his nails black. "Skylar. Ran into your girl the other day."

Souta's gaze ran up and down Skylar, assessing him before he reached out and took the offered hand. "Souta."

"I'll let you guys get back to your date. Just wanted to say hi." He tucked a hand into his jeans pocket, which I thought would have been impossible, but apparently not. "But if you guys want more company or anything, I'm just over there with my friends. Feel free to come over."

Following his finger back in the direction he came from, I noticed a guy and girl sprawled on a fringed blanket, though I couldn't see much more than their dark hair.

Skylar waved as he turned and headed back to his friends, an oddly strong gust of wind swirling around us for a mere second when he turned.

"Damn, he's adorable." Grinning, Souta shook his head and pushed his brown-black hair back into place. "That's the friend you made the other day?"

I nodded, then shoved at my neon-red locks. "Yeah, and he's twenty-five, if you can believe it."

Souta's jaw dropped. "No way. He can't be much older than us."

"That's what he said. But did that gust of wind come from him? I don't think he's Elementum."

"It wasn't me, and it didn't feel normal. He might be a random." Leaning over, Souta dropped a kiss to the tip of my nose. "Either way, I'm glad you made a friend, hot stuff."

I wrinkled my nose up and grabbed a chicken salad sandwich.

As The Scribblers gave way to Liquid Bass, I pushed the containers away, too full to eat another bite. Souta packed what we hadn't eaten back into the basket as I watched the lead of Liquid Bass prance around the stage. While the music sounded great, the

116

lead didn't look entirely comfortable. He jerked, movements awkward and stiff.

"He's overthinking things." Souta shook his head and settled back onto the blanket with the food finally packed away.

"Doesn't he need to think about his movements? He has to plan them or something?" Since I tended to be behind a guitar when on stage, I never worried about moving around.

"Well, yes. You plan a routine, but that's not what this is. He should be just moving, letting the music guide him. Look." Souta pointed at the stage. "There. That motion should have been seamless, but he pauses just for a fraction of a second, thinking about what to do for the next move, giving it that jerky feel. Here, watch."

He jumped up, light as always on his feet, and did the same twirl the singer attempted, but with notably more finesse. I couldn't take my eyes off of him. With his fluid grace, he continued to dance, hypnotizing me and drawing the eyes of those people seated nearest us.

"How do you know all this?" I stared at him, amazed.

He shrugged, plopping back down on the blanket. "I've been dancing since I was three."

That made a lot of sense. He always had a natural fluidity when we played.

His movements had me wondering what he'd look like onstage. I'd been toying with an idea but wanted the boys with me. "Hey, what would you think about trying to do a few open mic nights or something?"

I thought we were good enough to develop a local following, and music was the only thing I'd ever wanted to do, anyway.

Souta leaned over and quickly pressed our lips together. "I think it's brilliant."

Excited, I kissed him in earnest, his tongue ran over the seam of my mouth, asking for entrance. I opened to him willingly. Our tongues danced as our hands wandered. Music swirled around us, feeding our passion. The cool rush of air against my lower stomach as the zipper of my jean parted slammed me back into reality. For fuck's sake, we were in the middle of the park, surrounded by people, and I was seconds from losing my clothes.

"Souta." My hand closed over his, preventing it from finding its way into my panties. Souta stared at me with glazed eyes, then blinked a couple times.

"Sorry." He grinned ruefully. "You make me a bit crazy."

He removed his hand and eased to the side as I fastened my jeans back up. "Mutual."

We both sat up, and Souta held his arm out. I scooted until I sat between his legs, my head on his chest. His arms wrapped around me, and I tried to calm my raging hormones.

"We'll talk to Brooks and JJ," Souta murmured into my ear. "But I think we should go for it."

Excitement shot through me, followed closely by worry. If I wanted to be in the public eye, I couldn't ignore the fluctuation in my abilities. God forbid I had a surge on stage. Time to buckle down and figure out what the heck happened, so it didn't happen again.

NINE

I sighed and tossed my phone down onto my bed, watching as it bounced perilously close to the edge of the floral comforter. Looking at the online archives wasn't working. There was nothing at all about sudden surges of power in young Elementum.

The incident at school continued to hover in the back of my head, haunting me, not to mention the fight that caused the surge and the underlying reason. In more ways than one, I hurt Souta, and the temptation to plead with Mr. Rhinehart for a new partner nearly won. Souta was right, though. He needed to learn to handle things like this better, and that wouldn't happen if I gave in every time he got his boxers in a bunch.

Half of the time we spent in English was dedicated to working with our partners on the project, and Dane agreed to meet in the library during lunch as needed. If we needed to meet outside of school, we'd figure that out.

I wished I could figure out how to get Dane to stop pushing Souta's buttons. During class, he got very handsy with me by running fingers along my arms or touching my face or hair. He didn't touch me unless he knew Souta was watching, and I asked him to stop. Partly because it made me uncomfortable and partly because he did it on purpose. So far, Dane had ignored my request to stop, but he did focus on the work. And I suspected getting a good grade was almost as important as pissing off my boyfriend.

Even after school, the question of my power surge remained. I couldn't let it go, and I didn't want to. What if it happened again? What if it happened at a completely random moment when I wasn't even using my power? What if it happened when I was at the mall or somewhere similarly public, somewhere human?

Sitting up, I admitted defeat. I would need to go to the Tabularium. Maybe I could find something in the restricted archives.

Guiltily, I stared at the closed closet doors, then

knelt and pulled my suitcase from under the bed, careful to listen for footsteps as I did. I'd been here a while and never put my clothes in the dresser or closet. The boys didn't know, they thought my stuff was in the bathroom. Even my brushes and makeup remained in the container I used for traveling under the sink. I couldn't bring myself to settle in and make myself at home the way everyone wanted. Flipping it open, I pulled out a slim black, off the shoulder sweater and slipped it on over my pink tank before shoving the suitcase back under.

Just in time as my door cracked open, and Souta peeked his head in. "Hey, hot stuff. Whatcha up to?"

I sauntered over to him, pulled the door open, and stepped out of the room and into his embrace. Warm, comforting, and strong, I loved the way his arms felt around me. "I need to go to the Tabularium, to see if I can find any answers about what might have happened at training the other day. Wanna join me?"

His dark brows rose as the corners of his mouth twitched up in a grin. "And how were you getting there without me?"

Slipping out of his strong arms, giddiness flooding my system as I sauntered down the hall. "Oh, I thought I'd do it the old-fashioned way." With an exaggerated sway to my hips, I started down the stairs. "You know, stick out a bare leg, shake my ass and—" When I glanced over my shoulder, Souta watched me with hooded eyes. My stomach flipped, and heat buried the giddiness. "Whistle." I blew him a kiss.

He growled as his foot hit the first step and mine hit the last. I ran for the door. Grabbing my black motorcycle boots, I managed to slip them on before a firm grip landed on my hips and drew me back against a hard, muscled chest.

Hot lips skated over my neck, trailing tiny kisses down to where my neck and shoulder met. I tilted my head to give him more access as I wrapped my hands around his where they rested inches above my throbbing center. The sharp sting of teeth caused me to moan and arch against him. His warm palm pressed against my lower stomach, pushing me against a hardness restrained by jeans. Shifting my hips slightly, I teased us both and leaned hard against him.

He sucked at the spot he'd bitten as his fingers drifted lower. My legs turned rubbery as his hand slipped into my jeans—I failed to notice or care he'd opened. Reaching up, I tangled my fingers in his dark silky hair and gripped his head, needing something to hold me up as badly as I needed his mouth to continue its passionate torture of my neck. He moved his assault up my neck as his nimble fingers found the edges of my pink lace panties. Teasing the edge of the lace before moving lower, his hand cupped my core, the thin layer of lace the only thing separating us. I moved against his hand, aching for his touch, panting with need.

Teeth nipped my earlobe. "Mmm…" he whispered into my ear. "Look at that. Soaked through already, hot stuff?"

As his fingers caressed the fabric, I whimpered and pressed against his hand.

He cupped me back and ground his length against my ass, steel in need of release. "Feel what you do to me?"

Elements, I did, and it made me even hotter. I whimpered again, fingers curling into his hair as I thrust my hips against his obvious need. With another growl, he roughly shoved aside the thin barrier that blocked his fingers from my core and plunged in.

Need flooded me, and I cried out. "Please."

I writhed and panted as he thrust his fingers in over and over. His length pressed firm to my backside, feeding my need.

"Please. Please. God, please." I'd never felt anything like this before, and I never wanted it to stop.

More, I needed more, something else. My body tightened as it barreled toward some unknown edge.

"That's it, hot stuff." The warm breath against my ear was too much, and I moaned as he spoke, head falling back against his shoulder, red strands plastered to my cheeks. "Fuck, I wish Brooks could see you. So damn hot right now."

My body shook as he plunged his fingers in again, hard, then pulled one back out.

Lost in sensation and need, his thumb flicked my clit as his finger gave a shallow thrust. "Come for me, hot stuff."

My world exploded as I cried out and came apart in his arms. His fingers continued their rhythm for a couple more seconds as I shook, pulsing with aftershocks, before he pulled them out, arms wrapping around me tightly as I slumped.

His hardness poked into my ass, and I realized he didn't get the same release I did. I started to slip my hand between our bodies, but he captured it.

"Nuh-uh." His voice throbbed, tone lower than normal. "I'll deal with that later. This was all about you." He pressed a kiss against my temple, then wiped away the strands of hair plastered there. "A little lesson on what happens when you try to tease."

We stayed there for a few more moments before my legs felt strong enough to hold me.

Straightening up, we finally headed to the garage.

We'd barely gone the five feet out the door and down the walk to his sleek, black sedan when his mom pulled up and exited her little pumpkin-orange hatchback hybrid.

My eyes widened, pulse fluctuating wildly, as I realized how close we'd come to being caught in the foyer.

What the fuck was I thinking, letting him do that where anyone could walk in? A few minutes more, and his mother would have walked in! If they got upset and kicked me out, I'd have nowhere to go. I couldn't afford to upset or piss them off.

Souta and I got carried away in the park and, now, in the foyer. Is this what he wanted? Me to be the wanton, little, sex kitten? Fuck. Why was I even worrying over this? I had other things I needed to figure out, like the power surge at school.

"Where are you two off to?" Souta's mom asked with a tired smile. She'd been called into the hospital overnight for an emergency, so she hadn't gotten much sleep.

"Heading over to the Tabularium." Souta wrapped an arm around his mom's shoulders and side-hugged her. "Just looking up a few things. You look exhausted, Mom. Why don't you get some sleep? I'll take Sera out for dinner tonight."

His mom gave a nod, eyes already half-closed as she drifted to the door, graceful as always.

He leaned into me as we continued toward the garage. "Damn. That was close. Imagine if she'd walked in on us."

That was the problem, I had, but I couldn't dwell on it.

More and more, I've felt out of sorts. If we'd been caught, it would have made me feel more off-kilter. I barely recognized myself anymore and didn't know how to keep my boys and my family while still finding my way back to who I used to be.

Then again, who I used to be was cold and closed off. Did I even want to?

"Seraphina!" Jolted out of my thoughts by my full name on Souta's lips, his hand brushed the small of my back. "You okay?" His brows drew together as he popped open the passenger side door for me. Nodding, I smiled at him. "I called your name three names, hot stuff. You sure?"

127

How lost in my head did I get? "Yeah, just got lost in my thoughts."

"Okay." He raised an eyebrow but dropped a kiss on my temple before he rounded the car, and we both climbed in.

This would be my first trip to the Marysville Tabularium, but most of them were similar, and I'd been to others. The drive was short and quiet. Neither of us needed to fill the silence with meaningless chatter, though we did start dissecting a couple of the songs we listened to on the way.

Souta turned into a circular red-brick drive that allowed access to a parking area off to one side. We parked and headed to the door. The Tabularium was a two-story, pale gray Victorian home with bright, royal-blue accents and no signs or any indication of what it was. One of the few Elementum buildings not hidden from human eyes, it went largely unnoticed by most people, mistaken for a residence.

My eyes searched over the structure for the mark I knew would be hidden somewhere. The sign of the Elementum, a simple compass with line symbols at each direction. After a moment, I found it, hidden among the carvings decorating the molding of the porch that run the length of the house. After knocking, the door opened to reveal a woman with blond locks caught up in some kind of complicated knot on her head, clad in simple, dark-wash jeans and a pink blouse.

"Afternoon, my dears. Your cards please." I pulled my card from the wallet attached to my phone as Souta did the same.

They seemed to be blank, silver cards, but when she passed her hand over it, the familiar compass symbol flared then disappeared, responding to whatever minor power she used. She nodded and stepped aside to let us in. I slipped the card back in my wallet, knowing how important it was. The cards were used in all Elementum establishments that weren't hidden as a way to ensure a random human didn't stumble upon our secret.

We stepped into the foyer, a simple white affair with a pale wood door, likely a coat closet, and a long cherry wood table.

"I'm Archivist Gabby," the woman introduced herself as she led us through an archway to the left of the door, "I'm sure you know the rules, but I have to go over them, anyway."

"Nothing is allowed to leave; this information is too sensitive to risk. Gloves must be worn at all times. We've managed to make most of the manuscripts stable, so it shouldn't be an issue, but the precaution is still necessary. No pictures, videos, or recordings of any kind are allowed. The restricted works aren't in these rooms but are available upon request."

She spun to face us as we entered the main room of the Tabularium. It would be a historian's wet dream, completely restored to its original Victorian style, not to mention the shelves of yellowed scrolls and parchment carefully stored behind glass. Or the hand-bound leather books with gilded decorations on the covers. "The shelves are labeled by the sections, I hope you find what you need, dears."

"If you need assistance with something, you need only ask." Gabby pointed to an old-fashioned intercom system on the wall. "Simply push the button and call. One of us will come."

With a nod and a smile, she strode out and left us alone among books and scrolls older than I wanted to contemplate.

I glanced around, trying to figure out where to start.

Another archway, opposite the one we came through, revealed another room filled with shelves and more books. A fireplace at one end, flanked by several Victorian chairs and a couple side tables, made a cozy reading area.

Souta headed for the box containing gloves set on

a long table and slipped a pair on before handing me a pair. "Where should we start?" We tugged on the gloves, and he strode over to the shelves, fingers running along the spines without actually touching them.

"I have no idea. Anything about power, I guess?" So much of our history remained myth or hearsay, verbal histories handed down until someone finally wrote it out, then recopied it through the years until the archivists figured out how to preserve them. I didn't know how they did it, as far as I knew it was a secret known only to them.

"The creation myth?" Souta suggested.

I shook my head; I'd already looked at the creation myth, and it didn't hold any answers.

His finger paused on a book before pulling it out. "Someone needs to figure out better titles. *Elementum Society: Its Beginnings and Traditions: An in-depth look at how we began.* Really? Lot of damn words that don't make me want to read this."

When he glanced back at me, I shrugged. "Might be worth a look, but I'm guessing it won't be much help."

I joined him at the shelf, looking over the titles until one caught my eye. *What Can We Do? A Historical Look at Elementum Abilities.*

Pulling it carefully off the shelf, I headed toward the long table and pulled out a chair to sit. "I'm gonna check this one. You're right, though. Seems like they were all titled by the same guy."

Souta joined me, the society book still in hand.

"Might be worth a look." He reached over, ran his fingers through the soft strands of my hair before gripping my chin and turning me toward him for a kiss. "We'll find answers, hot stuff. They're here somewhere."

My gut churned. What if we didn't find answers? Would I be a danger to the guys? Shaking my head, I put the thoughts from my mind and focused on searching for answers.

Two hours later, we weren't any closer to answers. We'd moved to the other room, and my stomach interrupted our silence with a loud growl.

Carefully, I rolled up the untitled scroll I'd found regarding *great power* and glanced over to find Souta grinning at me. My stomach emitted another growl as our eyes meet and neither of us could contain our giggles.

Closing his book, Souta bounced up and grabbed my hand, pulling me to my feet.

"Apparently, I'm neglecting you." His grin made me feel a little better about not finding answers. We still had a lot more books and scrolls to search, but we needed a break. "I'll text Brooks as soon as we decide where we want to eat."

Nodding, I picked up the scroll and the book to return them to the shelves we'd found them on.

"Archivist Gabby," Souta spoke into the intercom, "we're heading out now, ma'am."

She must have been around the corner or down the hall because she met us just outside the rooms. "Did you find what you needed?" She smiled again, and I noticed how genuine it seemed. Too many human librarians had fake smiles. I shook my head. "Oh, dear. What were you hoping to find?"

"Information about power fluctuations, or sudden increases in abilities," Souta replied for me. "We're working on a school project."

A lie, smoothly told, and one I was thankful for. I didn't know that I wanted any more people than necessary knowing what happened. Needing Souta's touch, I reached out and laced our fingers together.

"Next time, why don't we check the restricted

section?" Archivist Gabby offered. "I think I recall something in there about fluctuations of power."

"Thank you, that's a great idea." Souta gave her his killer smile as he wrapped an arm around me. "Come on, hot stuff. You need feeding."

TEN

"Hey, firefly." JJ leaned over the back of the couch in the den and kissed my cheek. "I'm kidnapping you today."

Glancing up from the movie we were watching—one with plenty of things exploding even if I couldn't remember the name of it—I smiled. After the failure of the Tabularium yesterday, I needed a release or a break or just to watch things blow the hell up.

I tilted my head to the side for a better view of those molten gold eyes. "Is it kidnapping if I want to go?" I reached up and pulled him down for a better kiss, firm lips on his.

A peck on the cheek wasn't going to cut it.

"I'm going with no," Souta piped up from where he sat curled around one of the huge overstuffed, fringed floor cushions. Since we were slumming it today, his black hair was all over the place, and he wore only a pair of low slung, plaid flannel sleep pants. "You're taking her for the day, right?"

"Yeah, I got plans for our girl." He waggled his eyebrows or tried to anyway. It ended up looking more like someone tased him. Failing to contain my laugh at his goofiness, he mocked glared at me, then stalked around the couch. "Oh, you think it's funny, do you?" He perched his hands on his hips and tilted his head, a black lock curling onto his forehead.

Holding my hands up in surrender, I shook my head, but he still looked so ridiculous I couldn't stop laughing. Gripping my waist, he lifted me and flung me over his shoulder.

"No!" My screech barely escaped through my laughter. "Souta, save me!"

Souta laughed. "At least let me kiss her before you haul her off to your mysterious cave."

As JJ spun around, I pressed my hands on his back to lift myself as much as possible to glare at Souta.

"Traitor," I muttered as he closed the distance between us.

"You look stunning as always, hot stuff. Even upside down." He pressed his lips to mine, his tongue demanding entrance, but the angle was too awkward to do more than peck. "Have fun."

Bounced out the front door across JJ's shoulder, I couldn't help but wish he was coming with us. Unfortunately, Souta had obligations. He'd promised his old dance instructor he'd help fill in at her studio today, since one of her teachers quit without notice.

Once we made it out to the driveway, JJ set me on my feet, where a vaguely familiar tan sedan waited. He opened the door as I pondered where I'd seen it, then it hit me. The first time I'd been to JJ's his father came home in this car.

"Where are we going?" I climbed in, and JJ closed the door on my question.

He rounded the car to climb in the driver's side before answering. "It's a bit of a surprise. You'll love it. I promise."

We headed out, and I let silence reign as I took him in. I loved JJ's style. It always seemed simple and effortless, but he looked amazing, with just a touch of class. Girls at school still craned their necks as he walked by, and he remained oblivious to his effect on them.

Today he'd chosen a pair of dark-blue jeans and a fitted, emerald-green Henley topped with a faux leather blazer/jacket thing I'd seen him wear several times. He'd tossed a green and black scarf loosely around his neck and wore a pair of black shoes that seemed too nice for ordinary sneakers.

Once again, I worried about being underdressed for a date. Mind you, I wore a lovely pair of black jeans, with no tears anywhere—which was a miracle in itself—a long-sleeved, flowy top with splashes of bright-purple, lime-green, and turquoise and simple black flats. But what if he wanted to take me somewhere nice, somewhere better than our usual haunts? Would my outfit be good enough? I'd needed to search to find the shirt I was wearing, and I couldn't remember why I'd bought it in the first place. It wasn't my usual style, but I figured JJ would like its large splashes of color.

It didn't take long to arrive at our destination, and I climbed out of the car, staring at the simple storefront windows littered with unpainted, stark white mugs, vases, and figures. A brightly colored sign proclaimed the place to be Art Spot, a stylized, neon bullseye standing in for the O. I had seen places like this before, where they held all kinds of little things you could paint, then take home. A hand slid into mine, and I grinned at JJ, the teeth sinking into his lip revealed his nervousness.

"After everything going on, I wanted to do

something relaxing and fun. You need it, I think. Hopefully, it's not too silly, or childish?"

Grinning, I wrapped my arms around his neck. "I love the idea," I whispered against his lips, his golden eyes widening. "Just don't expect pretty from me."

Kissing him, my tongue dived in to play with his for several minutes. I panted as I drew back, my insides tingling and my heart racing.

Forget about painting, I wanted to drag him back into the car, find a deserted parking lot and live out a few fantasies. And that scared me a little. The way they all drove me crazy enough to forget all common sense, it felt like I was losing myself in them, and I wasn't entirely sure I minded.

Swallowing hard at the direction of my thoughts, I turned toward the shop, hoping JJ didn't catch any hint of where my mind ventured. It wasn't their problem after all. I slid my hand down his arm, tangled our fingers together, and tugged him inside.

A young gal in paint-splattered jeans, T-shirt, and apron sat at a table with a mom and daughter. She glanced over distractedly as the chime on the door tinkled our arrival, not really focusing on us. "Welcome to Art Spot. Have you ever been here before?"

JJ nodded. "We're good."

Has he brought Sophie here before? Or does he just enjoyed coming in on his own?

"Great. Why don't you have a look around, pick out your piece, and I'll be right over with some supplies? I'm Marissa, if you need anything." Marissa returned to helping the mom and little girl at the table with her.

"Come on, firefly. They have some great stuff if you know where to look."

I let my eyes drift as he guided me toward a shelf near the back. The walls were lined with shelves, each one filled with random things. Mugs, plates, bowls, and containers of all kinds and sizes fought for space with whimsical trolls, animals, and knickknacks. Bins with smaller items sat on a couple shelves, and I wondered what fun little treasures they hid.

Then I looked at the shelf JJ aimed for. Really looked. Most of the shelves contained similar items to the others around them, but the top two shelves held very different items. These items were bigger, more complex, and elaborate than the cute little bits of whimsy everywhere else.

I scanned over them, looking for something I could paint that I wouldn't ruin too badly. A rearing horse stood next to a noble knight and his lady fair. A majestic lion rested next to an elaborate pirate ship.

And behind it, I found the piece I wanted to paint, no matter how horrible it might end up. Nearly on tiptoes, I reached up and grabbed the dragon, complete with flames shooting from its mouth.

"Nice choice," JJ said as he stepped up next to me, a large mug in his hand.

I'd thought he would choose one of these more elaborate pieces, but I realized something like a mug would give him way more artistic freedom.

"Come on, I have us set up over here." He jerked his head toward one of the tables.

I followed him, noticing paints, brushes, and cups of water laid out and waiting.

My curiosity must have shown on my face as we sat down on paint-spattered chairs, because JJ grinned when he glanced over at me. "I've been here a few times. Marissa was distracted by the group she was with when we came in, so she didn't realize it was me. And I know my way around."

"JJ!" Marissa strolled over to us, eyes fixed firmly on my boyfriend and a wide grin on her face. "I'm so sorry, I didn't realize it was you."

She stepped close, one arm starting to wrap around his shoulders.

Nope. Not happening. Snagging his hand, I laced our fingers together, smiling even as I glared at the way too forward bitch. She needed to go find a man of her own.

My completely oblivious boyfriend just grinned at her as he waved away her apology. "No worries. I knew where everything was." JJ wrapped an arm around me. "I'd like you to meet my girlfriend, Sera."

The gal's eyes flattened, and her smile froze. "Lovely to meet you. Let me know if you have any questions."

Not a chance in hell, bitch.

JJ turned away from her, to snag two aprons off the table. He gave me one and pulled the other over his head, before picking up a brush to hand me. "Watch your brush size, especially when it comes to the smaller details, and you'll be fine. What color are you planning to paint it?"

From the corner of my eye, I watched Marissa slink away and restrained the smirk trying to break through. I bumped JJ's shoulder with mine as I pulled on the apron, then dipped the brush into the deep crimson paint. "Red, of course."

"Right. What was I thinking?" He dropped a kiss on my lips before he selected a brush of his own. "Want my help?"

Since I had no idea where to even begin, I nodded.

"Okay, start with your base coat, not too heavy. Better to do a couple thin coats rather than one thick one."

"Like nail polish," I mused as I leaned into him.

"Yeah, I guess." He laughed, the sound sending a shiver through me.

I loved his laugh.

"Work on the big areas, and I'll help you with the details, Okay?" JJ's arm wrapped around me for a quick squeeze, careful not to jostle me, as I held the dragon steady and applied paint to his chest. He picked his mug up and painted a strip of blue around the edges.

For several minutes we worked in comfortable silence, both lost in our creations. Absorbed in trying not to screw up the beautiful piece, my brain was quiet for the first time in weeks. Peaceful, in a place of no worries or fears, I relaxed completely. Now I could see why JJ loved art so much, especially if it helped him like this.

Wet on my nose yanked me from my meditative state, jerking me upright. "You were way too relaxed, firefly. I thought you might fall asleep." He choked the words out around fits of laughter. My nose still felt wet. Trying to cross my eyes to see what he'd done, I caught a hint of red.

"Did you paint my nose red?"

JJ hid his brush behind him and continued to grin at me. "No idea what you're talking about, Rudolph."

Deliberately dipping my brush into the red paint, I lunged at him, "Oh it's on." Wielding my brush like a tiny sword, crimson paint dripped from the tip. He tried dodging, but I was faster and managed to leave a huge red stripe on his cheek. His chair rocked precariously. We grabbed each other before he toppled over. Once steady, his arms came around me, and he gave me a quick kiss.

I glanced over at the mug he was working on, thankfully not seeing any random drops of red. He'd painted it a vibrant lime green with bright blue strips at the top and bottom, Sophie was written in pretty, flowy lettering across the middle. The beginnings of a hot pink flower indicated he wasn't done yet.

It was a bit on the eye-searing side, but from what little I knew of his sister, she'd love it. Our embrace lasted a little too long for comfort in a public place, so I wiggled out of his arms.

"How's Sophie doing?" I retook my seat and went back to my dragon.

"She's adjusting." He rinsed the red paint off his brush and switched back to his neon palette. "It's so new. It's hard for her to figure out everything she needs to do now to stay healthy and make sure she gets her insulin dosage right and all. My folks are beating themselves up for not noticing the symptoms sooner despite the doc telling them it happens a lot. But there's an obvious change in her that's nice to see."

He finished off the flower he'd been working on and set down his brush after rinsing it. "Come on, let's see about the details on your dragon, then you can see her yourself. We're going to catch a late lunch with her and my folks after this."

I tucked the hand not holding the brush under my thigh, so he wouldn't see it shake. Lunch with his family? Crap, I wasn't prepared for this. They were the most normal people in the world, and I needed them to like me. They wouldn't deny our Genus, but I wanted them to be okay with me being in a relationship with their son. And I was far from normal.

Thankfully, I dressed to please JJ. Hopefully, that would help.

Burying my nerves, I let JJ guide me through adding in details on my dragon as he finished off a few more embellishments on Sophie's mug. Twenty minutes later, we left our pieces with Marissa for a final firing or whatever needed to be done to them. Honestly, I hadn't bothered to pay attention to her words after JJ said he would pick them up later, my nerves still getting the better of me.

As I climbed into the car, I had to slide my hand under my thigh again, so JJ wouldn't see me tremble. Despite having spent time over at his place, I'd only briefly spoken to his parents a few times. I knew his sister a little better, mostly because she came into the studio when we were playing.

We pulled up to a place I'd seen but never been, one of those chain family places, which meant keeping all Elementum stuff under wraps. This would be an ordinary, family lunch. Elements, could I do ordinary?

I wiped my sweaty palm on the seat as JJ rounded the car and opened the door for me to get out. He laced our fingers together, and we headed inside. I worried my hand would betray my nerves, but he didn't seem to notice anything wrong. Inside, sunlight streamed in from the huge windows, making the hand that shot up and wave easy to see.

My stomach flipped as we made our way to the table. Halfway there, I let our hands slide apart, my feet dragging. Stopping back a few steps, JJ hugged Sophie, then ruffled her dark auburn hair, messing up the long ponytail she'd pulled it into. He laughed as she scowled at him. Dressed in a pair of pale blue pants and soft pink tee with a smiling, sequined watermelon on it, Sophie's outfit made me feel better about my own casual choices.

He greeted his parents with smiles and a kiss on the cheek for his mom. In a pair of jeans and a navy-blue polo, JJ's father looked so much like him it was easy to imagine what JJ would look like at that age.

His mother, on the other hand, her stunning features set her apart. Her dark auburn hair curled around her chin, perfectly styled without a single hair daring to fall out of place. Wide eyes the same golden-brown as JJ's with long lashes and perfectly arched eyebrows. She was around my height but carried a little extra weight. Even so, in a simple pair of jeans and a plain yellow top, she screamed elegance.

Just like Sophie, they looked so ordinary, like every other family in the brightly lit restaurant.

What was that like, to be so... normal? So close? I tried to swallow around the lump in my throat. Could I do this? Could I fit into their world? What if I said something offensive or did the wrong thing? Would they hate me? Want me to stay away from JJ? I didn't understand family dynamics.

I cared way more than I ever thought I would about him, about all of them. The idea of not being with them made it difficult to breathe. Fuck, it would kill me.

"Firefly?" A soft touch to my cheek jerked me out of my head. My gaze caught the concern in his golden-brown eyes. "You okay?"

No, I wasn't, but how could I tell him that?

With a deep breath to bury my nerves, I pasted on a smile. "I don't know." I spoke quietly, not wanting to upset his family. "But I'm not ready to talk about it right now, okay?"

JJ's fingers toyed with strands of my hair. "Sure. Whenever you're ready, firefly."

He pressed a kiss to my temple, and we took our seats. Right now, I might not be okay, but I would be, eventually.

Until then, well, I would keep going the way I'd been.

ELEVEN

School on Monday was a welcome distraction from the stress of the weekend, and I hated thinking of it like that. Spending time with Souta and JJ on our dates was amazing, but I felt like my skin was too tight these days. Or maybe, more accurately, the sensation I was in someone else's skin.

For the first time in two days, it felt like I could breathe. I'd slipped on a pair of torn black jeans, a long-sleeved shirt covered in sugar skulls, boots, and my jacket this morning. Officially I'd been a part of the guys' Genus for almost a month now, and I thought things would be different. I thought we'd end up seamlessly fitting together, working without much thought or effort. It would just happen, like the magic binding us together. Only it wasn't.

Maybe it should have, would have, if I were at all, even remotely, normal. But how was it supposed to work with three family guys and a girl who'd been largely isolated her entire life? Granted, I'd never minded being alone, until I met the guys. Now I had to work hard to fit into the boys' lives and families. Well, two of them.

Brooks still hadn't introduced me to his family, though I had an inkling why. I caught the impression his family demanded his time. Neither Souta nor I had seen much of him over the last week unless it was at school. Speaking of which...

I scanned the courtyard around the front of the school for his adorable blondness.

"See him?" Next to me, Souta's dark gaze also scanned the courtyard.

In a pair of fitted jeans and a red Henley topped with the lightweight black jacket he usually wore, Souta looked so damn good I nearly reached up to check if I was drooling.

Fellow students lounged around on the concrete steps or planters filled with hardy green plants and lackluster, brown mulch or leaned up against the red brick of the building. The overcast sky didn't allow any sun to warm us but, thankfully, no breeze came along to freeze anyone. A couple students sat at one of the two round stone tables and bench combos, books open, and papers spread across the rough gray surface. Through the glass double doors, more students milled around the dull lockers, or strode through the main hall, obscuring the hideous crusader on the floor. The volume level was ear-splitting, with a million conversations, videos or music on people's phones, and the slamming of car doors filling the air around me.

A shiver ran down my spine as I caught sight of those weird, cold eyes again at the edge of the student parking lot, Chester. This time they seemed to be boring a hole right into my soul. Wrapping my arms around my waist, I turned and rushed toward the school to get away from his gaze.

"Sera!" I dimly registered Souta calling after me, but I needed to get away from that odd stare. A few steps from the doors I slammed into a hard-muscled body. Arms grabbed me when I stumbled, preventing me from falling to my ass on the concrete. My heart seized in panic until I looked up to find my savior was Dane. Panic turned to irritation when his gaze flicked over my shoulder, and his hands drifted down to my waist to pull me against him.

"Shame when a guy can't manage to keep his girl."

Dane's snarky voice grated on me. "Good thing I'm here to take proper care of her."

Oh my god, how did any girl fall for this guy's crap? I put a hand to his chest and shoved, hard, but his grip on my waist tightened, making it look more like I was grinding against him.

A familiar, angry growl came from behind me.

Breathe, don't let the fucker get to you, Souta. He's just pushing your buttons.

I didn't say that, though, too busy still shoving against Dane and trying to wiggle out of his hold.

"Fuck off, Hicks! Stay away from my girl! And from Brooks, for that matter!"

What the fuck did Brooks have to do with anything? Shoving and wiggling weren't working, and whatever material the puke-green sweater Dane wore was made off, it itched against my palm like a million ants. Time for more extreme measures.

I ran my hand down his chest, watching through narrowed eyes, and he grinned wider over my shoulder. "Mmmmmmm, yeah, feel something you like, baby?" Dane practically yelled the question, and fire raced through my veins.

My hand found the edge of his jeans. In one swift move, I grabbed his nuts in a vise grip, heated my hand, and twisted.

"Ah!" Dane screamed as he doubled over, hands dropping away from me like lead weights.

I shoved him backward, and he screamed again as I finally released him.

Loud, cackling laughter drew my attention.

Glancing over my shoulder, I found Souta with tears of laughter streaming down his delicate face. He took a couple deep gulping breaths and wiped his eyes, then strode over, eyes shining with laughter as he took in Dane, still doubled over with a hand on his family jewels.

Souta settled an arm around my shoulders and pressed a kiss to my temple. "Come on, let's go find the others, hot stuff."

As we headed inside, my gaze drifted to where I had seen Chester, but the spot was empty of people now. A shudder ran through me at the memory of his stare.

"Hey. What's wrong, beautiful? Cold?"

My head jerked around at the familiar southern drawl. With a huge grin, I stepped out from under Souta's arm and into Brooks' waiting ones. Not wanting to bring up what I was sure was a ridiculous reaction to a stranger I latched on to the excuse and nodded. He tucked me into his side as Souta joined me in the warm embrace. Brooks' arms wound around both of us as he pressed kisses to the tops of our heads. A hand ran down my back, another pair of lips pressing a kiss to the back of my neck.

"Okay, firefly?" JJ murmured against the sensitive skin of my neck, sending shivers of desire plunging downward.

Standing here, in my boys' embrace, any agitation and unsettled feelings I had melted away. "Yeah, just Dane being a dick."

JJ growled, but Souta laughed. "Don't worry, our girl took care of him."

JJ lifted a questioning brow, but then the bell rang.

Gently batting at arms, it started to feel a little ridiculous, how I reacted to a simple stare, I wiggled free of the circle of boys. Giving myself a shake, I shot them a grin. "Come on, we don't want to be late." Turning, I strode toward history.

Halfway through history, a note slipped onto my desk.

Let me know if you need me. Our spot is always open. B.

Warmth spread through me, my heart melting a little at his concern. How had I ever thought I stood a chance at keeping them away?

As the bell rang, I gathered my stuff and met the

boys outside the door. I tangled my hand in Brooks' golden curls and tugged him down for a quick kiss.

"Thank you. I will," I whispered against his lips before kissing him again and letting go.

He nodded, turned, and headed down the hall toward his next class.

Brooks still felt like the biggest mystery of the three of them, but oddly enough, I also felt like I'd connected with him first and in a more intimate way than either Souta or JJ.

JJ pecked my cheek. "See you at lunch, firefly," then took off, too. Left with Souta, we linked hands to head to math. Oh, joy.

Souta was the only reason I ever made it through math without detention. Mr. Thompson wasn't a bad teacher, but we rubbed each other wrong. Old fogey. Today I managed to keep my mouth shut, my head down, and my thoughts worry-free all the way up to the bell.

Next, I headed toward Genus studies alone since Souta's class was on the other side of campus. On Friday, Ms. Gallup told us to meet her out in the courtyard for today's class, so I headed that direction. Pushing through the doors, I came face to face with those odd, cold eyes again.

"You." His voice washed over me, a warm rumble

most would have found sexy but grated against my senses.

I backed the fuck up until I felt the cold glass of the door against my back. Objectively, he could, and did, turn heads with his black hair, fit body, and a face straight out of the movies, but those eyes.

They froze my insides.

He leaned in, and I swallowed hard. "I can feel it around you, practically pouring off you. I can almost smell it."

My self-preservation instinct screamed at me to kick him in the nuts or tear his eyes out and get the hell away, but my body wasn't cooperating. He breathed in deep, as if committing my scent to memory, and it was enough to unfreeze my body. My knee came up and slammed into his crotch, sending him to his knees with a cry.

I groped for the door handle, finding it seconds later and falling through the door, right into Ms. Gallup.

"Sera, dear, are you okay?" She glanced at the door and scowled when she caught sight of Chester on his knees. "Dammit, did he bother you? I don't know why Scholae Jones insists on letting him hang around. He'll never find what he's looking for here."

Ms. Gallup steadied me, then reached around to open the door. "I suggest you leave."

Her voice held steel, and I wasn't at all surprised when Chester stood, hunched in discomfort, and hobbled off without a backward glance.

After giving the guy some time to clear out, Ms. Gallup patted my shoulder. "Come on, dear. You're going to enjoy today's lesson, I think. We're studying the creation myth, and I thought everyone might like the chance to be outside among their elements."

I loved Ms. Gallup. She was tall, probably around six feet without the heels she always wore, with a body that seemed a lot healthier than the stick figures I would often see on women of her height. Short, brown hair curled around a delicate face with wide hazel eyes. And she carried herself with a regal bearing that put me in mind of queens of old. On my first day, she told me she didn't give two figs about what the records said, and that everyone should be able to start with a clean slate.

Without hesitation, I followed her outside to where the others waited not too far off in one of the larger side areas. Unlike the one I found shortly after starting, neatly tucked out of sight, this one was open to the rest of the courtyard.

A wide courtyard held a tiered water fountain. In the center rose a marble basin filled with dry leaves and branches, waiting for the kiss of flame. Below, a basin filled with water fed from smaller fountains bursting up around it. Benches surrounded the fountain, with wide planters that overflowed with flowers and shrubs, settled between them. From each planter rose stone pillars with flags at the top, to catch the wind. Several large shade trees protected the area from any onlookers.

The court of elements.

Not every Illustratio possessed one, but in my opinion, they should. When the basin in the center of the fountain was lit, you could practically feel the Mother's blessing. All four elements existing in perfect harmony. It's clear why it was a favorite of the students. Everyone took seats on the stone benches, Ms. Gallup turned to me. "Would you like to light the brazier for us, please?"

Hell, yeah!

Pulling my lighter from my pocket, I flicked it and ran a hand over the flame to capture it. I tucked the lighter back into my pocket, playing the flame over my other hand and concentrating on feeding it enough power to ensure it caught the brazier on fire. It didn't seem to be doing anything at first, so I fed it a hint more power.

As I tossed it toward the pile of tinder, my insides lit on fire, racing through me and bursting out the tips of my fingers. The small ball of fire erupted into a huge sphere and hurtled at the brazier.

Around me the other students screamed, a few falling backward as if trying to get away, though they sat far enough to be safe. I watched, frozen, as the branches caught with a roar, the flames shooting into the sky ten feet before falling back and simmering.

"Well, that was quite a display Sera." Ms. Gallup wiped her forehead with a small smile.

"I - I'm sorry." I barely got the words out, still unable to move. All around me, the others were taking their seats again, several shooting glares my direction. More than one muttered, "Show-off," could be heard.

Only, I didn't mean to do more than send a small ball of flame at the brazier, certainly nothing like throwing a monster fireball. And that drop in power just before the surge? I never felt anything like it either, as if the flames actually raced through me.

"Let's try to keep it smaller next time, dear." Ms. Gallup dismissed the incident and turned to address the rest of the class.

Unable to dismiss it so easily, I barely heard any

of the lesson because my mind was trying to figure out what happened.

Between the incident with Chester and the huge ball of unintended flame, I wanted nothing more than to curl into Brooks' lap and let his calm soothe me or get lost in music with Souta or watch JJ perfect a piece of art. Thankfully, lunch was next. When the bell rang, I snatched up my bag and tried to take off, needing my boys more than ever, but Ms. Gallup stopped me with a hand on my arm.

"This isn't the first time this has happened." She said it as a statement rather than a question. It didn't surprise me she knew about the incident in P.E. I nodded. "It's unusual for someone so young to display such power."

Nature didn't like being told what to do. It took a lot of effort for any of us to manipulate our element, and real power took years to cultivate. Also, being part of a Genus was supposed to temper our powers to give us more control, not less. I shouldn't be able to do the things I had been doing.

"Do you know why it's happening?" I shook my head and wished I did. "I'll look into it. I've never heard of anyone's ability fluctuating like this, but you never know."

"Thank you." I didn't stop myself from throwing

my arms around the ample woman and giving her a quick hug before racing for the door again.

"For what, dear?" She called after me. I skidded to a halt in front of the door and glanced back over my shoulder.

"For trusting that I didn't do it on purpose," I called back and slid through the door.

The halls were too crowded for me to run full tilt for the cafeteria, so I settled for pushing my way through as fast as I could.

As if he knew I needed him, I found Brooks first. He opened his arms while I remained several feet away, and I launched myself at him. Burying my face in his chest like always, I breathed him in. We stood in silence for several minutes while I let myself freak out. Footsteps approached, and Souta and JJ joined us, but they didn't reach for me for once. I might have broken down if they had.

"Do you need privacy?" Brooks whispered the question, but I shook my head.

Everyone would know by now, anyway. I pulled away, leaning up for a gentle kiss before turning to the others. JJ pulled me in for a tight hug and a tongue-thrusting kiss.

When it was Souta's turn, he held me against him

for a moment before tangling his hand in my hair. "You okay, hot stuff?"

"I'll tell you about it once we get our food."

After a quick trip through the lunch line, we all sat, and the boys looked at me expectantly.

I started with Chester.

"That fucker!" Souta exploded the second I stopped talking. "I swear if I see him again, I'll—"

Brooks' hand on his arm stopped Souta's tirade before he could build up steam.

Souta sank back into his chair. "Weirdsville needs to find somewhere new to hang."

Silently, I agreed with him but doggedly continued by telling them about the ball of flame and how the fire felt like it was actually inside me. I prayed they wouldn't walk away as I talked. I should have known better.

Brooks leaned over the table to kiss my cheek. "Don't worry, beautiful, we'll figure out what's going on."

"Yeah, we will," Souta replied as he dug into his food.

I sent a prayer to the Mother that they were right.

"I think we need to go back to the Tabularium soon." When they all nodded in agreement, I pulled my phone out, eyes catching the waiting text.

Dane: Where the fuck are you?

"Shit," I muttered and stood, gathering up my nearly empty lunch tray and backpack. "I'm supposed to be working with Dane in the library today. I gotta go."

As I kissed them, the boys all scowled but didn't bother to try to stop me.

I dashed to the nearby library, thankful enough of lunch remained to be productive.

Slowing as I neared the door, I pushed through quietly, spotting Dane at one of the wood tables, a book open in front of him, pencil tapping against a notebook as he stared at his phone.

I set my backpack on the ground as I plopped into the hard, wooden chair. "Sorry, something happened last period, and I forgot," I whispered frantically as I shot Dane a glance and grimaced.

His face was pulled tight, and he glared back at me. "You know, I do actually give a shit about my grade on this."

Pulling out my materials, I murmured, "I really am sorry. What happened, it was—" I tried but failed to suppress the shudder that ripped through me.

The anger visibly drained out of Dane, and he nodded. "I thought maybe you were still pissed about this morning."

Dane wiggled in his seat as if the memory pained him, and the reminder of what happened sent anger flooding through me.

"Speaking of which," though I still whispered, the angry tone couldn't be missed. "What the fuck? You were deliberately baiting him. I might have to work with you on this, but that shit needs to stop. I don't understand how any of these other girls could stand you long enough to give you the time of day."

Dane slouched into a lazy sprawl and sent me what he must have thought was a sexy look. "I guess girls just know hot when they see it, and once they have the best, well…"

Dane shrugged but tensed when I burst out laughing. A glare from the librarian, a stuffy, white-haired older lady, had me swallowing my remaining laughter, but I barely held back the grin.

"Wow. You are as stupid as you look." I tilted my head and watched as he racked his brain for some explanation for my reaction.

We'd had enough time working together that I was pretty sure I knew exactly what happened in the past. Leaning forward, I rested my elbows on the table and met his confused gaze with my serious one.

"You care about your grades, a lot. Most people don't care like that, in my experience. How many girls barely did any work? How many did you threaten to report before they just seemed to fall into your lap for an easy fuck? After all, if you were distracted by sex, you wouldn't notice how little they did. Since you were the one doing all the work. And what happened after, with their relationships…" I shrugged. "I'd bet they were either already on the rocks or it was guilt that ate at them. You were just a toy for them to use for an easy A."

He gaped at me as my words sank in, but I didn't want to hear anything he might say in response. "Now, let's get some actual work done, shall we? Because I do care as much as you do."

TWELVE

As I stood on the porch of Michael's house, I wanted to throw up. Dad's house, I meant. Using the word, even in my head, still caused me some trouble. After I knocked, the door swung open, and Kelly smiled wide as her gaze took in my torn black stockings, leather shorts, and sheer purple shirt over a black tank.

"Come in, sweetie." She stepped aside to let me in.

Following her into the living room, I racked my brain for something to say but came up blank. Michael rose from the couch as we entered and crossed the room to envelop me in his arms. I kept the hug short, stepping back after only a couple seconds. As I sank into one of the chairs, I noticed a leather photo album on the coffee table. Kelly followed my stare.

"I didn't know your mother." She reached for the album, turning it over in her hands. "I only moved here a couple years ago. Michael found this hiding away on a shelf and was introducing us." She held it out to me.

Hopefully, she couldn't see how my hands trembled as I took it from her. Her eyes met mine over the album. I don't know what I thought I would see there, but I didn't expect the sympathy or compassion. She laid a hand against my cheek for the merest moment, then sat in the other chair.

The idea of seeing my mom for the first time sent my stomach spinning, and I was grateful she realized how difficult this moment might be for me. Michael sank to the couch, patted the cushion next to him.

"Why don't you come over here, and I'll show you Cali."

Silently, I shifted to the couch and handed over the album once I sat next to him. He opened it, flipping the pages too quickly for me to get a real sense of anyone present in them.

"Your mom was a real spitfire." He spoke absently as he searched the album pages. "We both lived too far out to be bused daily into Illustratio, so during the week, we lived in the Ignis dorm. Basically, we grew up together. Can't count the number of times the two of us, and Hugh—a terra—ended up at the nurse during training. Ah! Here it is!"

The page he stopped on held only one picture. The rest of the page was decorated with confetti, stickers, and balloons. "The three amigos take on the world!" was written in gold ink above the picture with a date underneath.

In the picture, two guys stood with their arms around a girl, all three smiling broadly into the camera. They appeared young, not much older than me. The guy on the left was a young Michael. The one on the right possessed short blond hair, spiked up, and twinkling blue eyes. He held himself with a confidence bordering on arrogance.

As handsome as the young men were, the woman between them held me captive. Flame red hair fell in gentle waves around a delicate face. Bright, mischievous green eyes stared me from behind black, cat's-eyeglasses. Curvy legs ran for miles from under a skirt so short and tight I didn't think I would even dare to wear it. Curvy body, barely covered, and creamy, pale skin.

Elements! Mom was a bombshell! From the

suitcases next to them, it seemed they were going on a trip.

"Myself, obviously. Hugh Sage. And your mom, Cali." Michael tapped each person in turn. "Thick as thieves the three of us. I think this was the last picture where we were all three together. Newly graduated and off on a trip to Europe courtesy of Cali's parents."

"Her parents?" More family I hadn't known about? If I had grandparents, why wasn't I sent to live with them? Had they not wanted me?

Michael's smile dropped. "They were killed in a car accident about a year after this photo was taken."

"Oh." That explained a lot.

Heaviness fell, and I struggled to find a way to lighten the atmosphere.

My eyes fell on the third member of their little group. "I bet you and Hugh have some great stories about Mom. Any chance of meeting him?"

It felt like the air grew heavier with my words. "I'm sorry, honey. Hugh died about four years ago."

That didn't help the situation. The silence grew more awkward, and the longer it stretched, the more uncomfortable it became to say anything. And *I'm sorry* didn't seem like the right words.

"Well, clearly, we're in need of cookie relief." Kelly

stood from the chair where she'd been a quiet presence and bustled into the kitchen.

Michael softly smiled at her when she returned with a plate of chocolate chip cookies.

"No milk?" he teased.

"You know where it is!" She winked at him before turning to me. "Did you want some milk, Sera?"

Her attention on me was nice but odd. "Yes, please."

"Michael, why don't you get us some milk?" He laughed and went to get our milk.

Picking up a cookie, I continued to stare at the picture of my mom as I ate.

From my side, Kelly's voice was soft and unobtrusive. "You have Michael's eyes, but you look like your mom, too. The nose, lips, and chin are definitely from her."

"Do I?" I wondered aloud, reaching for another cookie.

With my focus solely on the picture, I failed to notice the lit candle until I put my fingers in the flame.

"Ah!" Yanking my fingers back, I whimpered.

A gentle touch on my wrist drew my attention back to Kelly. "Let me."

She drew my hand close and rested her fingers above the sore area.

A moment later, blessed cool rushed over the burning sensation, washing it away.

I guess that answered my question on if she was human. "Aqua?" I asked, just to be sure.

Kelly nodded. "Yes, and a cooler."

Michael rushed in, a tray with three glasses of milk sloshing around dangerously gripped in his hands. "What happened?"

"It's nothing," Kelly reassured him as she released my hand. "Seraphina had a little accident with the candle, and I took care of it."

Michael released a sigh of relief as he set the tray down on the coffee table and sat.

"Hey, Dad," a voice called out. "I need—"

I looked up when Ash's words cut off abruptly, only to meet his scowling stare. "What is she doing here?"

Though his words were at a reasonable volume, I couldn't mistake the wariness lacing his voice. From his reaction, I began to doubt if I would ever have a relationship with the man who is my half-brother, and I wasn't entirely certain I wanted to be close to such a hothead.

His gaze fell to the album open on the table. A frown pulling his face down as he strode forward.

Michael cut off anything he wanted to say. "Don't you start, young man. Sit down."

Ash shot me a wary look as he took a seat.

Michael flipped the album around, tapping the picture again. "You know who that is." A statement rather than a question.

Ash nodded. "Sure, that's Hugh, River's stepdad, and Cali. Right? The girl you two used to hang with." He looked up, brow furrowed as he met his dad's gaze. "You two used to tell all kinds of stories about her, but she died a long time ago."

"About eighteen years, actually." Michael waited a heartbeat.

What was he doing? What did he think this would accomplish? At first, Ash's face was uncomprehending, then after a moment it lit with understanding, and his gaze shifted to me, assessing.

"Cali is her mother?" His voice rose in shock. Kelly reached over and patted my shoulder, but we both stayed silent.

For my part, I didn't want to disrupt them or remind them I was here.

"You've heard the stories, heard how she was and what she believed." The wariness left Ash's face. "In those moments when the grief was the worst—" Michael took a breath when his voice cracked. "When I was buried so deep, I couldn't see those who needed me. When I wanted nothing more than to join your mother, Cali was there." His finger tapped just below Cali in the photo. "She's the one who pulled me back, who reminded me I needed to live, that I had people who needed me. That you needed me. And, yes, a couple of those moments turned physical, but that's all they were. I was too buried in grief, and she would never have allowed more. I don't owe you an explanation, but I hope understanding will open your heart."

Ash's gaze shifted to me, the wariness slowly fading but acceptance still elusive.

Not that I blamed him.

"It's a lot to think about." Ash's measured words were careful, but at least he didn't seem hostile anymore. When he glanced over at me, I felt like a specimen under a microscope.

Finally, he nodded and looked down at the album again. "Has he told you about the time they went to the shore and your mom's dare? Hugh loved to tell that story."

I shook my head and watched Michael blush as Ash launched into a retelling.

"They were, seventeen, I think. And they'd gone to the shore for the first weekend of summer break. Of course, they weren't the only ones who thought that was a good idea, so the place was crowded when Cali dared Dad to wear her bikini top for half an hour. Her bright pink, string bikini top." He paused for a moment to let that sink in, and my eyes widened at the image in my head. "Of course, Dad objected to the length of time, but agreed to do it for fifteen minutes, which happened to be enough time for the girl dad had a massive crush on to walk by and see him. He tried to rip it off the second he spotted her, but his time wasn't up, and Cali and Hugh made him keep it on when the girl walked up and asked him about it."

Grinning at Michael, Dad, he continued, "Apparently, our dad was quite the conversationalist with girls, because all he could do was stammer and stutter, then say, 'Just thought I'd see what it was like'. The girl found the idea of Dad wearing girls' clothes weird and took off."

I cracked up at the images playing through my head, Ash and Kelly laughed, too, even as Michael chuckled at the three of us. "Alright, enough of that."

Ash shook his head. "Nuh-uh, there are too many more stories."

He shared a couple other stories Michael and Hugh had told him over the years. The mood in the room was cautious, careful, reserved but the hostility Ash first brought with him no longer existed.

Hearing tales about my mom was bittersweet. I'd never known her, but now I had an inkling of the woman she'd been, and the mother she might have become. Was it possible to miss something you'd never had?

By the time I left an hour later, there was a tiny flame of hope we might someday be able to have a real relationship as siblings.

Michael didn't live too far from Souta, so I had walked over, wanting the time to bolster myself. Instead, I'd nearly managed to work myself up to the point of bolting. As I left and turned toward Souta's, I debated calling any of the guys for a ride, but my phone rang before I could.

Looking at the lit-up screen, I saw Dane and sighed. What the fuck did he want?

"What?" I barked out the word as the wind rushed past.

The cold, damp air held little discomfort when I could simply heat my body. Zipping up my leather jacket, I tucked my hands into the pockets and heated myself to stop the cold from biting so badly.

"I had some thoughts about our project." No flirting, no sexy preamble, just straight to business. He'd been a bit more like that since I'd told him off in the library. "And a couple things I need to run by you, but I can't do it over the phone. Can you meet me in the park around the corner from Souta's in like ten minutes? I don't have long, but this won't take more than ten or fifteen minutes."

I didn't really want to, but I would pass by the park, anyway. "Yeah, but it needs to be quick, and no funny business." I let steel into my voice so he would know how serious I was.

"Yeah, yeah. I don't have long, seriously. See you in a few." He clicked off, and I stuffed my phone back in the pocket of my shorts.

The park was between Dad's and Souta's, and when I saw the familiar lake, I turned in, only then realizing I didn't know exactly where to meet Dane. The problem solved itself a minute later.

"Sera!" I turned to find Dane dashing toward me and braced myself for one of his disgusting comments or come-ons, but it never appeared.

Instead, Dane waved a DVD case at me. Breathing hard, he came to a stop and shoved a hand through his blond hair. "Thanks for meeting me." His eyes lit with excitement. "My folks were going through some stuff and unearthed this."

When he waved the DVD again, I grabbed it so I could see it better. A colorful cover with the words *Romeo and Juliet.*

"I was curious, so I watched it, and I think this is what we need for our performance."

My brows lifted. "We weren't in this play."

"No, I know." Dane shook his head. "That's not the point. You need to watch it. What they do with the play, I think we need to do something like that. It's really different."

"There are so many versions of this. What makes this one different?" I didn't want to watch some crappy remake of a story about two teenagers being complete idiots.

"You have to watch it. Trust me." As if he knew that was never happening, his face twisted in a frown. "Okay, trust my need to get an A on this project and watch it."

That I could trust.

Sighing, I took the DVD. "Fine."

With no desire to extend this little scene and not trusting him to behave now that business was done, I turned to leave.

Two steps later, a hand gripped my upper arm lightly, and I looked back.

A red flush crawled up Dane's neck. "I…" He swallowed hard. "I thought a lot about what you said, in the library. And what you were too nice to say. And how you've been calling me out on my behavior from the second we were paired up. I just…" His eyes shifted to the side, focusing on a very interesting blade of grass at our feet. "Thanks, I guess." He shrugged, the flush crawling over his cheeks.

Before I could respond, a new, familiar voice interrupted us. "Sera?"

A weary Skylar walked down the path. His blue gaze darted between Dane and me, then focused on Dane's hand on my arm. "Everything okay?" He stepped closer, eyes narrowing. "I wouldn't mess with her, man. Her boyfriend's something else."

Holding back the giggle at the thinly veiled threat, I slipped my arm from Dane's barely-there grip and shook my head.

Dane muttered, "She's something else," barely loud enough for me to hear as he turned and left.

I turned toward Skylar, wondering where on earth he'd come from. "Everything was fine, but thank you." I held up the DVD. "He was passing this on for me to watch." Not able to stand the curiosity another minute, I asked, "How come I always run into you here?"

"I live in one of the houses near where we ran into each other the first time." He grinned as he jerked his head toward the path around the lake.

"You own one of them?" I didn't think people so young bought houses, did they?

Skylar chuckled. "No. I live with my grandmother. It's her place. I'm just there to help her out." His gaze drifted around the park slowly. "I'm here a lot, in the park I mean." Tucking his hands into the pockets of black skinny jeans, he refocused his gaze on me. "I've always been drawn to this place, to nature in general. Something about it—" He trailed off with a shrug.

The mention of our first meeting reminded me of our discussion that day. He looked calmer, but I knew how deceiving that could be. "How are you doing, you know, after your breakup?" Asking felt weird, but so did ignoring it.

The peaceful expression on his face dropped away as he kicked at the grass. "Alright, I guess. I know it takes time, I just," Tears shimmered in his eyes as his breath hitched, "I just want it to stop hurting already."

Wanting to hug him, but uncomfortable by the

thought, I placed a hand on his arm. He didn't notice, though.

"It was my own fault, really. I was so tired of hiding, of feeling like his dirty little secret and being only his good friend to everyone he knew. Four years of promising me he was nearly ready, that we could tell everyone soon." Tears slipped down his cheeks, his eyes unfocused as he talked, and I thought he might have forgotten I was even there. "Every day I got more impatient, more discontent. And I should have kept my mouth shut, should have buried those feelings like I'd been doing, but no, instead I had to confront him, yell at him, issue a stupid ultimatum I didn't even get to see through because he ended things then." A crow's caw startled us both into jumping backward. Skylar swiped at his wet cheeks. "Sorry, didn't mean to bring my issues to you."

"It's okay. I think you needed to talk about it. Why not a friend, right?" At least it felt like we were becoming friends. I hoped we were, anyway.

Skylar smiled, small but genuine. "You're right. And I don't have many friends left now. Oh!" His eyes widened, and he pulled a paper out of his pocket. "I'm glad I ran into you, actually." He held the brightly colored paper out to me. "There's this place, Thorium, which features local bands and the like.

Some pretty damn good indie bands there, especially on Fridays. You should check it out."

I took the flyer, noticing the graffiti-style art on it, and read the times for live performances. At the bottom of the page, a note about open mike night caught my eye.

"Oh, hang on a sec." The flyer was yanked out of my hand, a pen appearing from some hidden depths in Skylar's tight jeans. He flipped the paper over and scribbled something, then handed it back.

When I looked, I saw a phone number.

"If you decide to go one night, text me. I'll meet you there." His gaze lifted to the darkening sky. "I should get home." He fluttered his hand in the general direction of the cluster of houses.

A sudden gust of wind rushed by, the cold bite reminding me I dropped my heating. With a shiver, I tucked the flyer into my pocket. "Yeah, me, too. Souta's expecting me."

He grinned and strode off.

Heating myself, I turned toward Souta's house, ambling rather than hurrying. Before I reached the house, I needed a few more minutes to think things over and the questions that would follow.

I still didn't know what Michael wanted from me, or what I wanted from him. The whole idea of family felt so detached from who I was, and now, I needed to find a way to be part of more than one. How did others do this? The connection I had with Michael seemed strong, and despite his initial reaction to me, the same strong connection existed with Ash. But I felt more comfortable with people who didn't demand anything emotional from me, Skylar being one example.

I'd begun to think of him as a friend, the first real one I'd had in a long time. Maybe it wouldn't be as hard as I thought to find my place among my family, both blood and Genus.

THIRTEEN

The walk back to the house should have given me plenty of time to sort myself out. It didn't.

By the time I arrived home, my thoughts were more jumbled, my emotions all over the place. Michael, Ash, the boys, the boys' families. So many people, too many people. People I needed to keep happy, to be okay with me, so I could stay with the boys. So, I could stay here and be normal for once.

Normal. I never realized how much I craved that.

Even though I continued to feel pulled in a million different directions, I was going to try my best. Mother, help me. Sending up the small, simple prayer, I walked into the house. It felt empty, since Souta was at the dance studio again, helping out.

Part of me wanted to go over and watch him interact with the kids. Since that day in the park, when he told me he danced, he took me to the studio occasionally, and I loved seeing how much his enthusiasm for dance inspired the little ones. Watching him dance wasn't bad, either.

"Oh, Sera. What good timing." Akiko, Souta's mom, smiled as she entered the hallway from the office she shared with her husband.

I froze, one foot in midair in preparation to ascend the stairs. Lowering it, I turned to face her fully, a small, half-smile appearing automatically in response to hers. I often felt drab next to her. Even now, on her rare day off, in a pair of slim fitted black slacks and ruby-red, wraparound blouse, with her long, glossy brown-black hair pulled into a simple ponytail and no makeup on her delicate, Asian features she exuded elegance.

"I have something for you, dear." She waved me into the office.

Following her, I tracked her movement as she crossed the room to a small closet where something in a garment bag hung from the door. The shop logo on the bag was unfamiliar, but I wasn't surprised, still being so new to town.

"It might be a bit presumptuous of me, but I saw

this and couldn't help but think how lovely you'd look. You never know when you might need something a little fancy."

My insides froze as her slender fingers undid the knot in the bottom of the bag with ease. The outfit tumbled out of the bottom, at least the skirt portion, and my eyes widened. My heart raced as she lifted the bag off the dress. Every muscle in my body tightened up as I clamped down the urge to get out of there, as fast as possible.

Even I could admit the dress before me was stunning. It was a deep, emerald-green color with golden flowers embroidered over the whole thing and gold trim sparkled along the edges. The straight skirt appeared to fall below the knees, the sleeves little more than a cap on the shoulders. The collar stood straight up, and the dress appeared to wrap around to the side, secured with elaborate, golden pieces I didn't know the name for. A slit ran up one side of the skirt, stopping before it could become indecent.

I had seen dresses like this before, but as an orphan girl living out-of-school dorms, it was so far from my station and style, I never contemplated wearing one. The expectations that come with a dress like this dried my mouth with fear.

My eyes darted to Akiko. A wide smile lit her face

up. This woman did so much for me over the last few weeks. She took me in, giving me a place to stay, and helped me heal.

And that was only the beginning.

Despite my discomfort, I would find an appropriate place and time to wear her gift. With any luck it would be a short event, so she could see me in it, then I could quickly change. I owed her so much; it was one thing I could do for her.

Slowly, I forced my hand out, fingers brushing against the satiny material. "Thank you. It's lovely." Not a lie. Firmly I wrapped my fingers around the hanger and took it from her, her smile got bigger as I draped it over my arm. "I'll be sure to find the perfect occasion for it."

"I know you will dear. Don't forget, dinner's at seven."

Exiting the office, I made my way upstairs to my room. The dress was a lead weight of expectation and obligation draped over my arm. Opening the closet for the first time since I moved in, I slipped the dress on the rod and gently slid it all the way to the back.

For a moment, I was tempted to unpack so I could hide the dress behind my own clothes, but the idea sent nausea rolling through me. I needed to find a way to get these emotions out, and for the millionth time, I wished I still had my guitar.

A few years back I'd found it in a random second-hand shop, shortly after learning to play. Surprisingly, I found playing helped de-stress me. Unfortunately, I left it out at the last Illustratio, and one of the munchkins tripped and fell on it. Broke the neck clean off, and the poor kid ended up with several jagged cuts.

My mind swirled and spun as I lay down on my bed, sending spikes of worry and fear through me. I wanted to turn it off, but I didn't know how. Shove it down or push it out, all those things people say weren't helping me. The worrisome thoughts kept resurfacing.

Had the dress been some kind of subtle message? Akiko didn't seem like the type, but I also couldn't see her coming out and telling me I needed to dress or act different. What kind of place or event would I wear something so dressy to? Would I have to wear heels with it? Fuck, I didn't know if I could walk right in heels. What about JJ's and Brooks' parents? What would they expect of me? JJ's parents were so different from Souta's, and I didn't know anything about Brooks' parents at all. My stomach clenched tight as I worried over who they might expect me to be.

Trying to release some of the tension inside me, I grabbed a pillow, shoved it over my face and screamed into it. A couple deep breaths later, I sat up and glared at myself in the mirror across the room.

What the fuck was I doing?

The dress was a gift. Nothing more.

I tried a few breathing exercises I'd read about, but my chest still felt tight. Noting the time, I slid off the bed and dug my suitcase out from underneath, needing to find an outfit to wear down to dinner that felt appropriate, but all I found was a knee-length black pencil skirt, a white blouse, and a pair of black pumps I didn't remember buying.

As I dressed, my gaze swept back to the closet door where the stunning, emerald dress hid.

Should I find something more colorful to wear? A glance back at my still open suitcase told me that wasn't likely to happen. My wardrobe held mostly blacks, reds, and a few whites. Nothing as bright or jewel-toned as what I'd seen Akiko wear.

Maybe I should just wear the dress, though it was a bit fancy for dinner. But then I'd have to act a certain way, walk a certain way, be a certain way. I would have to be... not me. The thought caught in my throat.

A glance at the hand-carved, wooden clock

revealed I was out of time, and I forced myself to leave the room.

I headed downstairs to dinner. We only ate in the formal dining room when his folks were able to join us. Their lives tended to be very busy, but they made time for dinner more often than I thought they would when I first moved in. Though I liked eating in the relaxed atmosphere of the kitchen better.

The formal dining room had elements you would expect it to have; beautiful, shiny, dark-wood floors, deep-red walls topped with crown molding, and elegant decorations on the walls. The usual stopped there. No fancy chandelier hung from the ceiling, no impossibly long table with candelabras. Instead, a simple, round, dark-wood table sat off to one side, leaving room for other tables to be brought in when needed, and a very simple, ordinary light hung from the ceiling. Despite the minimalistic decor, the room still sent me into a mild panic.

Souta's parents already sat at the table, set with simple white dishes, awaiting the delicious food I knew would soon be delivered. My stomach flipped when I realized Souta was absent. My spine stiffened, and I squared my shoulders. I took small, careful steps so the heels of my pumps didn't click too loudly against the floors. Souta's mom often wore heels, and hers never clicked the way mine did.

After I sat down, spaghetti and meatballs, completely homemade from scratch, appeared before us. Without Souta here to act as a go-between, I didn't know what to say to them, and we dug in without words exchanged.

After a minute or two, they talked between themselves, occasionally throwing a question my way that I responded to with brief answers or simple nods. Any confidence I possessed vanished in the unfamiliar situation.

The front door banged opened about halfway through dinner, and Souta rushed into the dining room. His dinner arrived at the table about the same time, but I barely noticed. My spoon clattered against my bowl when I dropped it, my mouth frozen open.

The form-fitting pants he wore left little to the imagination. He paired them with a black T-shirt, falling off one shoulder, and his hair fell into his face. I had to admit the disheveled look was sexy as hell on him.

"Sorry, I'm late. I got held up at the Academy." He slid into his chair and shot me a grin. "Hey, hot stuff. Have a nice time at your dad's?"

I nodded, but couldn't force myself to smile. Even his sexiness couldn't overcome my turmoil.

His brow furrowed, and he leaned into me, his hand resting on my thigh. "Everything okay?"

My appetite disappeared without any notice. I should have felt better with Souta here, but I didn't. And I didn't understand why.

"No," I whispered. "I think I need to be alone right now."

I wiped my mouth and hands on the napkin provided before I stood.

A hand clamped down on my wrist, and I looked down to meet Souta's beautiful, brown eyes, the question in them clear as a bell.

"I'm okay, I promise. I just need…" There was no way of putting this feeling into words. This need to bolt, not from them exactly, but the air in the room seemed to smother me, and I found it difficult to breathe. "Please." It was a mere breath, but Souta nodded and let go of me.

It was hard to walk out of the room at a normal pace, but the second I was out of their sight, I bolted for the room where I slept.

Sinking onto the bed, I berated myself for being a weak, silly idiot. The dampness on my cheeks meant my tears finally spilled over. Miserable, I curled into a ball and welcomed them. They drove the pounding thoughts away and let me fall into sleep.

———

The next morning, I woke numb. It was a welcome calm, but I couldn't let it stay and put the boys through that again.

After I pulled my bag out from under the bed and dug through it, I changed my mind on my outfit three times. Discarding the slacks, blazer, and tank outfit almost as soon as I pulled them out. I couldn't do preppy, no matter who might expect it of me. Finally, I settled on a black-and-red plaid skirt with black tights and a tight, long-sleeved black shirt with a rhinestone skull. Throwing on my leather jacket, I ran out the door to meet Souta and head to school.

He waited outside for me, and when he spied me flying out the front door, he opened his arms for me to dive into. The warmth and comfort I missed so much last night enveloped me with his hug. I still didn't know why I freaked out, but I was determined to do my best to move on. It would all get figured out, eventually. Until then I would keep my idiocy far away from the boys. No reason to worry them.

Souta dropped a kiss on my cheek. "Better today, hot stuff?"

I nodded. While it wasn't entirely true right this second, I felt better than I did last night.

"Good. Brooks called me last night when he couldn't get ahold of you. I told him you were having some personal time. He'd like to do his date this upcoming weekend."

"Sounds good." A thrill of curiosity muted my worry. I couldn't wait to see what Brooks came up with for our date.

FOURTEEN

With no idea what the plan for the day was, I dressed carefully and in layers. Brooks would be here any moment to pick me up for our date, but he refused to tell me where he planned on taking me. A knock at my door caught my attention, and I turned away from the mirror just in time to see Souta poke his head in.

"Wow, hot stuff. You look great." He slipped in and wrapped an arm around me. "Are you okay? You've seemed a little... off lately."

With Brooks arriving shortly, I didn't have time to get into anything now, and I was still reluctant. There were still things to work out in my head. What would be the point of telling him when it was still a confused muddle of relationship and family thoughts?

It would end up creating more problems than it solved.

"Just a lot on my mind. I'm fine." True enough.

"Okay." His tone betrayed his lack of belief in my non-answer, but he let it go. "Brooks is here."

He dropped a kiss on my temple, and I slipped out of his hold, brushing nonexistent lint off my short, black pleated skirt. Souta followed me out to where Brooks waited.

Brooks' face lit up when he spied us both coming down the stairs. He opened his arms, and Souta and I both stepped in. His arms curled around us, and we did the same, joining the three of us together in the embrace. I enjoyed affection from my guys, but this felt right in a whole new way.

Souta lifted his face, eyes meeting both Brooks' and mine. "Kiss."

The single word pulled us all in, and the next thing I knew, tongues were tangling, lips moving. I didn't know, or care, who kissed whom. It was odd and a little awkward since none of us knew what we were doing, but like the embrace, it was right.

So very right.

After a minute, though, our coordination fell apart, and I couldn't stop the giggle as we all pulled back.

"Okay, that was hot." Souta wiggled, trying to squeeze us closer together. "You two better go before I forget what you're supposed to be doing and drag you both upstairs."

I released the boys, and Brooks untwined his arm from Souta, leaving the other arm around me. After giving Souta a short, hot kiss that made me want to agree to Souta's idea, Brooks held the front door open and escorted me out.

In the front drive, a simple four-door, blue sedan waited. Given that I'd never seen it before, I concluded Brooks must have borrowed it from his folks. Only a few steps separated us from the car. I stopped and waited, knowing Brooks would open the car door for me. He always did, no matter who was driving.

He did the same for Souta.

"You look beautiful, as always," he murmured to me as I climbed in.

Before I could respond, he closed the door and rounded the car.

We headed off in silence.

Of the three boys, Brooks was the quietest. He didn't often say much, preferring to not draw attention to himself. His need to be in the background made me curious, but I wouldn't change his quiet nature for anything. He might not speak often, but he saw deeper than anyone I'd ever met. A comfort existed between us, one where words weren't needed. Despite that, I still wanted to know more about him.

"Tell me about your family?" I asked him since I had yet to meet any of his family. I wanted to be prepared when I did meet them. His grimace startled a blink out of me, thinking I imagined it.

"I would rather not." He sighed as he turned us onto one of the major roads. "I should, though, so you know when you eventually meet them."

Leaning the seat back a little I rested my hand on his thigh. His hand came down to rest over the top of mine, then he continued. "My folks are very different from me."

I remembered him telling me that when I had my freak out at school.

"They're extremely social and love to throw parties. My mom is in her element as a hostess and even does party planning for a living. Not weddings, of course, because, 'no one likes a bridezilla'. My dad is a good ol' southern boy in a suit. Put a beer in his hand, and he'll talk to anyone. He's a lawyer, so debating is one of his favorite things in the world, and he'll do it until he's blue in the face. My sister,

Sandra, is… a diva is the only way I can think of to describe her. She wants the spotlight. I'm amazed she hasn't already moved down to L.A."

He told me they were social people and loud, but until now, I didn't realize exactly how different they were from him.

His hand lifted from mine to scrape back his hair before settling on the steering wheel. "They don't seem to get privacy or boundaries. They push and push. There are no locks on any doors in our house, except the bathrooms and the front door, 'because we have nothing to hide.' They never ask me to do things, they tell. Obedience is expected to be absolute, not that they are unreasonable or ask for the impossible. I mean most people probably wouldn't care. Most of the time, it's just them forcing me to go to all their fancy events, family get-togethers, friend nights, and wherever else they tell me I need to go and need to participate in…"

I didn't dare move and barely dared to breathe. Never had he said so much at once, and I was pretty sure he'd forgotten I was even there. My question opened the floodgates, and they wouldn't close until he'd aired everything.

"… but most of the time, I feel like I'm suffocating when I'm at those damn events. It's not like I can find a book and a chair and read. If they'd let me choose the times I wanted to be there, or the events I was comfortable at, it would be different. But they don't, and they don't listen. They know best, and that's all there is to it. I haven't told them about Souta because I'm worried about how they'll react. Despite being Elementum, they had some friends who weren't really open-minded before we moved here. I just want them to hear me, to see me. Me. Not the person they want me to be, or the one they think I am."

His voice trailed off, but I didn't know how to react to what he said. Family was a puzzle I didn't know anything about, so any advice I would give wouldn't be worth a damn. The car jerked to the side of the road, then slowed to a stop.

"I'm sorry." He spoke to the steering wheel gripped tightly in his hands, and I barely heard the words.

I eyeballed the console separating our seats and made my choice without hesitation.

With one hand, I unbuckled my seatbelt, and with the other, I pried his fingers off the steering wheel and climbed over the console to straddle his lap. I wrapped my arms around him, hugging him tightly.

After a minute, he slumped into my hold, his face

buried against my neck, blond curls brushing against my shoulder. "I've ruined thin-things. I don't— I don't know what to-to say, to-to-to make—"

Lifting his head, I pressed my lips against his to stop his words, the sudden stutter surprising me. Nerves? Fear? Too many emotions?

I didn't know what the cause might be, but I knew one thing. I pulled back and cupped his face in my hands. "You don't need to say anything, just be you." His eyes met mine, so he could see the truth of my words. "Unless you want to share them, I don't need words from you. I've never needed them. You talk when you have something important to say. I love that about you."

Wait. Did I use the word love? My brain stuttered. I did. Now was not the time for examining my word choice, so I tucked it away for later.

"It should be me apologizing to you. I didn't mean to upset you with my question."

Brooks shook his head, hands resting on my hips. "Some things have been happening at home that has me on edge."

"Anything I can do to help?" I would do whatever he needed if it helped ease him any. Not to mention get him more time with us. It hadn't escaped my notice that we'd seen less of him in the last couple weeks than before. One hand lifted and pushed through my short hair to cup the back of my head.

"Just be you, beautiful. That's all I need." He gave me a short, swift peck before tapping my hip. "We should get going before a cop takes an interest."

Careful to not hit the horn, I moved back to my seat. We continued our drive, and I changed the topic of conversation to less stressful things, like his books. He loved to discuss them, and the fact I wasn't a fan of fiction in any form made for some fun debates as we drove. Several minutes later we turned off the main road into a dirt driveway.

As we turned a corner, I squealed, probably for the first time in my life, and the old house came into view, prettier than the pictures online, the historical society who ran the place obviously took pride in keeping it period-authentic. Vibrating with excitement in my seat, I barely registered the car stopping or Brooks getting out and coming around to my side to open the door.

When it opened, I flew out of the car and wrapped myself around Brooks. "I can't believe you remembered this place!"

Brooks chuckled as he squeezed me tight for a moment then released me. "You seemed excited about the chance to see it."

Grinning ear-to-ear, I grabbed his hand and dragged him toward the front door, practically bouncing while he paid the admission.

Our hands didn't separate as we wound our way through the house museum, reading the information plaques by all the displays.

When we got to the study, my gaze went straight to the glass displays in the center of the room.

Through most of the house, Brooks and I enjoyed the opportunity to debate a little. He would mention reading something about this or that in one of his books, which contradicted the information plaques. He must have been doing it to rile me up because he never put up much argument when I would correct him. Neither of us said a word as we approached the displays holding the old letters and diaries.

These diaries couldn't be read, of course. They were too delicate to handle from what I understood. However, the society had them open so people could at least read a little of them, and the letters were laid out page-by-page. I barely noticed when Brooks' hand left mine as I began to read through everything I could see. Several minutes later I looked up, realizing the warmth of him was gone, only to discover his entire body gone. My stomach flipped as I walked back into the hall, nearly crashing into my quiet guy.

"Hello, beautiful."

My brow furrowed as I noticed his hands held behind his back. "Where did you go?"

"I found their little gift shop."

His answer did nothing to clear up my confusion, and it must have shown.

He chuckled and pulled his hands from behind him, revealing the book he held. "It's a printed version of the one they have on display."

Throwing myself into his arms, I kissed him, soft and gentle. He pulled back, handing me the diary. I should stop being amazed at how well he understood me, but I didn't think I ever would.

FIFTEEN

The vibrations of the strings against my fingers felt like heaven, a calm I hadn't felt in weeks settling into my gut. My fingers moved, another stroke, more vibrations. The calm moved up my chest, my shoulders releasing tension I didn't realize I held. My eyelashes fluttered, and movement caught my attention. I let the chord fade and opened my eyes fully.

JJ walked slowly around a small chunk of some kind of stone I didn't recognize. His jeans were snug on his waist and thighs, and I could imagine them cupping his ass lovingly. The plain white tank, covered in gray dust, gave me a great view of his biceps as they flexed with his movements. Reaching up, I ran my thumb over the corner of my mouth, checking for drool because—hot damn.

As silence finally fell, he looked up, grinning wide when he caught my eyes. "Better, firefly?"

"Yes." I set the guitar on the nearby black metal stand and crossed the studio.

He tangled our hands together and drew me into his side, planting a kiss to my cheek. "You should have said something sooner. Take it home. It's yours. My folks will be fine with it as long as they know it's you who has it."

"Okay." My reluctance could be heard loud and clear, but arguing would be pointless.

When I told JJ at lunch about my old guitar and how it broke shortly before I left, I never expected him to haul me home after school and give me one of his. His stubborn streak was as wide as mine, though, and he knew how important something like this could be.

He released my hand and returned to walking around his stone.

Settling onto the bench in the studio, I watched him.

Half an hour later, a form began to take shape, though still too loose for me to say what it would eventually become. I loved watching him, but my fingers itched to play.

The door opened, and Souta ran in, brown-black hair going in a million directions as he slid across the bench to tackle me. "Hot stuff! I missed you!"

I laughed. "It's been like an hour since school ended."

Straightening us to a sitting position, I spied Brooks walking toward us. Something was off. Running my gaze over him, I tried to figure it out. His blond curls were in complete disarray, pale-blue shirt half unbuttoned and hanging out of his jeans, expression guarded, something I wasn't used to when we were all together.

"Everything okay?" I asked.

He nodded and leaned over to kiss me.

He'd had to go home and talk to his folks about something, some family thing or other. I wanted to pull him aside, ask him to confide in me, use me as a sounding board the way he'd let me use him so many times. Only I didn't know how to do it, or what to say to make him feel better. Nor did I want to push, so I let it drop when it became clear he didn't want to talk about it.

"Come on!" Souta bounced up, grabbed the mic from the stand, and spun. "Let's jam."

Oh, yeah, I was totally on board on with this.

I jumped up and met Souta's dark eyes, our grins matching as I picked up the guitar I'd used before. I whipped off a few chords of a song we'd been playing for a couple weeks, an original Souta and JJ put together months ago.

Brooks and JJ moved toward their instruments, flowing into the song without missing a beat.

I loved watching Souta when he performed, his moves all fluid grace and sensuality, his voice a perfect growl. He was made for the stage, and anyone who saw him could tell.

We ran through the song flawlessly and flowed into a cover of one of Souta's favorites, a tune from a Japanese artist I'd never heard of before. The beautiful, haunting lyrics echoed in the room, settling into my core, though I didn't know why. As the last of the song faded away, Souta tore his dark-blue T-shirt off and sent it flying into a corner of the room.

"Water." The single word rumbled from Brooks.

He rose and headed toward a pitcher of water and glasses sitting on a nearby bench I hadn't notice earlier. Then, my eyes caught on the small girl sitting a few feet away, long ponytail swinging along with her hot-pink-sneakered feet as she bopped to our music.

I set down my guitar and grabbed a drink before sitting next to Sophie. "Hey, how are you feeling?"

She shrugged, though her wide smile appeared genuine. "Okay. It's been hard to adjust, but I'm getting used to it." Her eyes drifted around aimlessly before settling back on me. "You all sound amazing. I've never understood why you don't play somewhere."

"That might change soon." I certainly hoped so, anyway.

"Good. I have to get back. I'm helping Mom make dinner." She waved as she rose and half jogged toward the door.

I waved back as she disappeared before moving to the bench I sat on earlier, trying to gauge the mood in the room. Souta plopped down next to me and leaned against my shoulder, watching Brooks and JJ as they chatted.

"Gonna try talking to them?" he asked.

Souta and I wanted this, but what about them? I didn't want to do this if we didn't do it together. It took me a moment to find my calm and soothe the fear and worries constantly assailing me lately. They had no place here.

A warm hand wrapped around mine, squeezing

gently, and I drew courage from the contact. "Hey, guys? We need to talk."

JJ's head jerked around, his eyes wide. Fear practically rolled off him.

Next to him, Brooks chuckled and patted his shoulder. "She didn't mean it like that."

JJ let out a relieved breath, his shoulders sagging as he walked over to us and settled on the floor in front of me.

Brooks did the same as Souta chuckled. "Maybe, find a better wording next time, hot stuff."

What was wrong with what I said? I shook my head and let the thought fade into the back of my mind for another time. "I've been thinking for a couple weeks... Well, longer than that honestly, because I've thought about it before I met you guys, but I wasn't entirely convinced until after I saw you guys play. Then, we played together and wrote that song."

Lips pressing against mine cut off my word vomit, and I raised my eyes from the concrete floor to see JJ smiling softly at me. "You're rambling, firefly."

Heat rose in my cheeks. "Sorry. Um, so, what I wanted to talk about was, how would feel about becoming a real band? Like finding actual gigs and stuff around here? I mean I love playing. It's all I've ever thought about doing, and Souta is practically made for the stage, and we sound friggin' awesome, even Sophie said so—"

The press of lips against mine cut off my babble again. I didn't know who stopped it, but I didn't care. Our tongues tangled, stroking, exploring. Brooks. My body heated, and I moaned, my hands reaching for hair to fist in and pull us together.

"Fuck, that's hot."

The words came from Souta, but I didn't register them. I scooted toward the edge of the bench, needing to feel more of Brooks. My fingers tangled in his curls, and I made a needy little whimper in the back of my throat. A hand settled on my hip, and lips pressed kisses along my neck, tiny nips following behind. My core began to ache, and hands wandered over my belly.

"By the elements, you guys are killing me." JJ's whispered words sent more need skittering through me.

I held out a hand in the direction of his voice, and a hand grasped mine. A body slid into the space between the wall and me, Souta from the feel of his body, and legs bracketed around me on the bench. His kisses and nips on my neck stopped, and his hands roamed up my stomach, brushing over my nipples.

Brooks broke our kiss, his hands skimming down my body, over Souta's hands, and stroked low on my belly. I wanted those hands lower. Over my pants, in my pants, I didn't care, they just needed to be lower. My eyes tracked Brooks as he moved to my side, his fingers dipping lower as he continued his ministrations. He leaned back, and Souta leaned forward, their mouths meeting with a flash of pink as their tongues tangled together.

I whimpered and spun my gaze to JJ, now on his knees next to Brooks, in front of me. I ached so badly my whole body felt as if someone lit me on fire. JJ released my hand, his own reaching up to cup my face, as he leaned in and devoured my mouth.

My own hands wandered, over chests, arms, tangled into hair, not a care for who it was as long as it was one of my boys. Brooks' fingers stroked lower, grazing the juncture of my thighs as Souta's hands found their way inside my shirt to play with my nipples. I moaned as Souta pinched my nipple, unable to stop myself from thrusting against Brooks' hand. My own hands fisted tight into the shirt I held, not knowing whose it was.

Souta flicked my nipples, and JJ thrust his tongue

in and out of my mouth as though fucking it. Brooks' fingers stroked firmly over my center, and my whole body tightened. I panted into JJ's mouth, moaning at the same time as my muscles continued to tighten from the stroking, flicking, and thrusting. I tensed until it felt as though I'd be torn apart.

On one loud moan, I exploded.

As I drifted back, I realized all the hands had stilled, falling away except for Souta's, which wrapped around my stomach to hold me on the bench. JJ sat back on his heels, panting softly, a prominent bulge straining against his jeans. I glanced over at Brooks, sitting on the floor next to me, to find him in a similar situation. From the evidence pressed against my back, Souta was, too.

Before my brain could process enough to offer to fix their issues, the door slammed opened, Sophie skidding through. "Dinner in ten!" she shouted and ran back out.

JJ's eyes caught mine. "Yes."

My head tilting as I frowned. Yes? To what? Dinner?

A finger stroked down my cheek, and I swiveled my head to gaze at Brooks. "He means we'll do it. It's a great idea. Let's figure out how to become a band."

SIXTEEN

Staring at myself in the mirror, I failed to recognize the person standing there. My stomach rolled. My mouth went dry. I hated that this happened every time.

Tonight, the sensations were worse. The air in the house felt heavy, like something hung there, waiting for the right moment to come crashing down.

Arms wrapped around my waist, making me jump a little as Souta pulled me back against his chest. He nuzzled my neck as his hands strayed to the buttons on the crisp, white blouse I wore.

I batted at them, rolling my eyes as I turned in his arms.

"I don't like it," he murmured into my ear before kissing the soft spot just below it.

I tilted my head to give him better access as he trailed kisses over my neck.

"Take it off." Steel laced his voice, sending heat pooling to my core. "It's not you. My hot stuff, my passionate Ignis."

"Dinner." The word came out on a moan when his fingers caressed my breast. "Your parents," I panted and gripped his hands to stop him from freeing buttons. Taking a deep breath, I told my body to calm the ever-loving fuck down and stepped back. "We should head down."

I smiled, hoping it didn't look as fake as it felt. With one last look in the mirror, I swallowed down the bile rising in my throat.

Souta was right. It wasn't me, but I was a guest in his parents' house. I needed to keep them happy, do the things they expected. When they were able to make it, his folks always looked so nice for dinner, and even now, Souta wore black slacks and an emerald-green button-down, though he left several buttons undone, the sleeves rolled up to his elbows. A pendant shone at his neck, one I hadn't seen before, and simple crystal studs sparkled in his ears.

He looked amazing and elegant.

Next to him, I felt like a cheap, dollar store doll

in the same white blouse, knee-length black pencil skirt, and plain black pumps I'd worn last time.

Souta crossed his arms over his chest, thrusting his bottom lip out in a pout I'd seen him use several times on Brooks. "You're no fun."

Grinning, I shook my head, knowing he wasn't serious.

"Well, come on then." He grabbed my hand and tugged me down the hall, the stairs, and to the dining room.

I stumbled after him, though I seemed to trip less the more often he did it.

My insides cramped as we walked into the formal dining room. Like last time, Souta's parents were already seated when we arrived, dressed as nicely as Souta and me. The table once more set with plain white dishes and cloth napkins, the light from the pendant lamp above the table glinted off the silverware.

My hand reached up to brush hair out of my face, forgetting I'd clipped it back to prevent that very thing. I dropped it quickly hoping no one saw my mistake. Souta skirted around me and pulled a chair out from the table, waiting for me to sit.

I still wasn't used to this part of the dinner ritual. Actually, there were a lot of things about the dinner ritual I still wasn't used to. Plopping gracelessly into the chair, Souta scooted it back in. Probably looked like some kind of albatross or something.

Souta's mom smiled at him as he took his seat. "Good evening, dear." She turned to me. "Sera, you look lovely tonight."

"Thank you," I murmured. The arrival of dinner saved me from trying to find something more to say.

The aroma wafting off the dishes made my stomach growl. A bowl was set in front of me filled with broth, noodles, and little meatballs. A plate set off to the side held a variety of things to add in. I recognized the pho despite it looking slightly different from the one time I'd had it. When I sipped the broth, the flavors burst on my tongue, and I needed to bite back a moan.

Thankfully, no one talked for several minutes as we all prepared our bowls and dug in.

After a minute, I glanced up to find Souta and his parents using chopsticks instead of the large soup spoons. I swallowed hard. I didn't know how to use chopsticks. With shaky hands, I turned to Souta, and he must have read my expression.

"Never used chopsticks?" He set his down, a grin spreading wide over his face. "No one expects you to, you know."

I nodded and went back to my dinner, but I couldn't help but think I saw disappointment in his eyes and his parents'. Maybe I imagined it, but maybe I should try, right?

"Sera, dear," as Souta's mom spoke, I glanced up, "we have something we'd like to discuss with you."

My stomach clenched tight, and I set my spoon down before my trembling hand dropped it. I couldn't seem to stop these sensations when they were around, and it annoyed me. I wanted to scowl but worried how Souta's mom would take it.

I took a deep breath, willing my hand to stop shaking and my stomach to calm.

"Really, Mom? Now?"

"Yes, now. When do you propose we talk to her? Time is running short."

Souta's scowl startled me. I'd never seen him scowl at his mom before. "You said you'd let me talk to her."

Souta's mom set her chopsticks down and speared him with a stern, disapproving gaze. "Yes. We did. Two weeks ago. You've failed to bring it up, so now, I must."

Souta sighed and flopped back against his chair, scowl now fixed on his pho.

His mother's face relaxed, and she turned back to me with a smile. "Now, we have an important event next week. An annual tradition, really. It's nothing to worry about, just a family affair, but we'd love for you to join us."

"I... um..." a response failed to appear as I tried to read between the lines. A family affair? What did that mean?

"Seriously?" Souta's angry tone caught my attention. "Why don't you tell her everything? She should know what she's getting into before deciding."

That didn't sound good.

"It's really not a big deal." She smiled again, peace and calm radiating off her.

"Not a big deal?" Souta turned to me. "This little family affair she's trying to get you to attend is a formal ball that our family does once a year. Each member of the family, every member of their Genus, their spouses or current others, their children attend. It's not by any means a small affair. Last year, there were nearly two-hundred people there. And by formal, I mean ball gowns, tuxes, and a fancy dinner with a million rules you don't know..."

The blood drained from my face as he spoke. Two-hundred people? My breath caught in my throat. Ball gowns? Tuxes? Fancy dinner? My stomach rolled, nausea churning. My eyes darted around the room as my breath came faster and shorter. I couldn't be here. I needed space, air. I needed to be alone for five damn minutes without the fucking walls closing in on me.

"I need to..." unable to finish my sentence, I stood.

It was all too much, and I strode out of the dining room toward the door.

My promise to Souta not to take off again without warning stopped me next to him for a mere second, eyes fixed on the floor in front of me. "I'm going for a walk. I need some air."

Once out of the room, I got all of three steps beyond the threshold before Souta stopped me.

"I'll come with you." Steel and command laced his tone, like it always did when he wanted to get his way.

This time, it wouldn't work. I needed some time alone, and I never seemed to get that around here.

I didn't even bother turning around. "No."

"Dammit, Sera, it's late. You shouldn't be out alone."

"You don't get it, do you? I need to be alone! Just leave me be for five goddamn minutes, for fuck's sake!" Praying Souta would stay behind, I stormed out the door.

Heading toward the park felt too weird this late at

night, so I walked along the streets. The bright lampposts would be safer, too.

A breeze rose as I walked, stirring the short hairs at the nape of my neck. I shivered in the cool air, wishing I'd thought to grab my jacket. With the full moon and the stars shining bright overhead, plenty of light illuminated the streets, but after a handful of blocks, an uneasy feeling settled into my gut.

I wandered aimlessly, for the most part, trying not to let thoughts of the family affair Akiko wanted me to attend consume me, simply following the brightly lit streets. A tiny part of me tried to push the matter, knowing I needed to deal with my panicky feelings and figure out why it happened, but I couldn't, not now. Reacting without thinking got me into a lot of trouble in the past, and until I managed to push the panic away, I would only be reacting.

As the cold settled into my bones, I heated myself enough to ward it off and kept walking. The heat pulsed as I feed it tiny bits of power to keep it at the right amount of heat. My feet began to ache. I pulled my phone from my pocket to check the time when a chill, having nothing to do with the cold night air, ran down my spine.

Uneasy, I checked around me, startled to realize I'd traveled farther than I thought. The lamps here were fewer and farther between, but I hadn't left the neighborhood. Deep, shadowy areas and little-used alleyways didn't exist here, and no odd, out-of-place characters lurked on street corners.

I shoved the unsettled feeling down deep and kept walking.

My mind circled back to the guys. They'd been trying so hard to make me feel like I belonged, but they didn't understand. Deep inside, I knew I belonged with them, there was no doubt we would find our way in our relationship, our Genus, and our future, eventually.

However, I was less sure about where I fit with their families and with my newfound one.

Being late, the stillness and quiet seemed almost unnatural, so when a loud crunching noise echoed through the night from behind me, I stilled. Thoughts of the boys and everything going on abruptly fled. I rubbed my hand over the thin material of the white shirt I wore. After a minute, with no more sounds breaking the night, I continued my walk.

My hand drifted down to the pocket of my skirt and wrapped around my phone as the sense of unease grew. A muffled sound reached my ears. Was it a footstep? My breathing quickened as I pulled my phone from my pocket. Staring at the screen, I debated who to call. My first instinct told me to reach out to the boys. Souta would come, but I wasn't ready to face him yet. Scrolling through my too-short list of contacts, I told myself to swallow my fucking pride and call him.

A contact I'd forgotten about caught my eye, and my finger hovered over it. It was the worst idea ever. He wouldn't come. He wouldn't care. Another barely-there noise reached my ears.

I hit the call button.

SEVENTEEN

"I swear to all the elements if this isn't some insanely hot chic looking for a booty call, I'm setting someone on fire." The voice growled over the line.

"Ash?" I hated the tremble in my voice, but I failed to realize how freaked I was until that moment.

A shuffle behind me made me jump, and my eyes darted around the street. My breath caught when I realized I didn't recognize anything. Where in the elements was I? How far did I wander? I was such a fucking idiot, wandering around, especially in this damn skirt and pumps.

"Who is this?" The short, sharp words sounded more alert than before.

A crinkle echoed down the street and pushed aside my hesitation.

"It... It's Seraphina." My voice lacked its usual snark and confidence as my breathing came fast and shallow.

"What the fuck?" he growled. "How the hell did you get my number?"

"Mi... Michael. Dad." I swallowed hard and spun, trying to get my bearings. "Just in case, he said."

Elements, was that movement? Calm down, Sera. You're freaking yourself out. Deep breath. Eyes peeled, I headed down the street, still unsure where exactly I would end up.

"What's wrong?" While still sharp, his words no longer held irritation but a wary alertness I found comforting.

"I think..." My voice trembled, and I took another deep breath. "I think I'm being followed."

"Where are you?"

I sent a silent thank-you to the universe and looked around for street signs. Not far from the corner, I dashed the remaining distance and read them off.

"You're close. Ten minutes, tops." A clinking sounded through the phone, and I hoped it meant he'd grabbed car keys. "Be right back." From the faintness of the words, I knew he called them out to someone else.

A sliver of discomfort ran down my spine at the thought I interrupted his night.

Cringing at my own weakness, I stumbled over the words to make things right. "Never... Never mind. I'll be okay, just being stupid." I hung up before he could answer, hoping he'd take my reassurances at face value. Stupidly, I closed my eyes, taking deep, even breaths to calm myself down. My mind kept escalating every little sound, the events that sent me out here in the first place not helping in the slightest.

Despite appearances, I wasn't defenseless. I needed to remember who I was and who I wasn't. Besides, it wasn't all that late, in reality. Dinner had been later than the previous time, but I hadn't exactly been walking around for eight hours or anything. Reaching into my pocket, my fingers brushed the cool metal of the lighter I kept there, reminding me of what I could do. Calmer, I decided to try retracing my steps.

The rumble of an engine echoed loudly down the street. I turned my head in time to catch the sleek, black motorcycle turn the corner at the far end of the street. As it drew closer, I noticed the flames painted on the sides and adorning the helmet of the rider. It pulled to a stop next to me, and the rider removed his helmet, holding it out in my direction.

"I didn't see anyone," Ash said, "but let's not take chances. Hop on."

"What about a helmet for you?"

"Nah," he shook his head, "I only have one. Let's go, we'll talk at my place."

Part of me hesitated. Ash wasn't acting upset, but he didn't sound concerned, either. I didn't want to hang around, and I didn't know how far I'd wandered, so I pushed that part of me down. Slipping the helmet on, I hiked up my skirt, climbed onto the bike, and gripped his sides.

I'd ridden on a bike once before, and the ride tickled those memories to the surface.

The guy who taught me to play the guitar—his name escaped me—had given me a ride on his bike once. I didn't remember being more than eleven or twelve at the time. I'd loved the freeing sensation then, and the years hadn't changed my enjoyment at all.

With no way to talk, the ride remained silent, giving me time to get lost inside my head again.

However, before a single thought could coalesce, we pulled into a small, two-story home.

Ash held the bike still as I used his shoulders for balance as I climbed off.

Unstrapping the helmet, I handed it to him once he swung off the bike.

He headed toward the front door, and I followed silently, not really looking around. I didn't know what to say or how to act. Shock still ran through me that he came in the first place.

Between the fear and the shock, I just wanted to collapse.

Lights flipped on, washing the dark hallway in a dim, pale glow. Ash tucked the helmet into a closet near the entrance, then led me into a large kitchen. Signs of a bachelor pad were obvious, even when I wasn't actually looking for them. Bare counters, dirty dishes in the sink, and not a single decoration anywhere.

"Sit." He nodded toward a table with mismatched chairs. I sat as he made his way over to a cupboard and pulled a mug down. "Coffee or cocoa?"

"Cocoa." I never liked the taste of coffee.

My shoulders slumped as I collapsed into a chair. Watching him as he moved around the kitchen, exhaustion moved through me.

"Nice tats."

I jerked my head up, not realizing I'd begun to doze. When I'd called Ash, I was surprised by how long I had been out. Between the time and the walk, it was a miracle I'd managed to stay awake on the drive over.

"What?" My brain failed to process his words.

"Your wrists." He pointed in my direction with a spoon.

Wait. When did he get a spoon?

"Oh." Brilliant conversation, Sera. Way to go.

Ash crossed the room, setting a mug with steam rolling off it in front of me. "They look great. Good quality work." Ash took a seat, another mug in his hand. "Didn't you just turn eighteen? They don't look fresh."

Confused and sleepy, I couldn't move past the fact he came for me and, now, wanted to talk tats.

"Why?" I asked and picked up the mug, blowing on it before taking a sip.

"Well, if you got them after you turned eighteen, they'd still be healing and really bright—"

"No," I cut him off. "Why did you come? You barely tolerate me."

Ash sighed and lifted his mug. "Not true."

Part of me wanted to believe him, but one good

moment at Dad's didn't negate his attitude before then.

"I tend to react first, and usually badly." He licked his lips, set his mug down, and turned toward me. "I owe you an apology. I was pissed at my dad for a perceived betrayal of my mom. I realize it's stupid since I didn't know her, but—" He shrugged as if words escaped him, but I knew exactly how he felt. "Is someone going to be looking for you? Where are you staying? The dorms?"

"Not anymore." I set the mug down. "I should call Souta, though. He's probably going out of his mind."

A question filled his eyes. One I would answer later.

During dinner, I set my phone on silent, and I had been too freaked out when I called Ash to notice anything, so seeing the missed call and text from Souta made guilt churn in my stomach.

Heart heavy, I made the call I should have made in the first place.

Souta answered on the first ring. "Thank the elements you're alive. Where are you? I've been going crazy with worry. I know things aren't settled between us, but dammit, hot stuff—"

"I'm fine." I cut him off before he could work himself into a lather. "I'm, well, I'm at my brother's."

Complete silence.

"Souta?"

"Why are you with that asshole?" His carefully measured words told me he wanted to shout and scream, but knew he shouldn't.

Telling him what happened over the phone would be a horrible idea. "I'll tell you when you get here."

Ash slid a paper across the table.

I looked down to find an address scrawled across it and read it off to Souta. It took a moment to reassure him, again, I would be fine until he arrived.

As I hung up, the question was still posed on Ash's face.

"Souta is my…" What should I say? My boyfriend? My Genus? He was both, but which was the right one in this situation?

"Souta. As in Souta Kurihara?" Ash sipped his drink, coffee from the smell.

"Um, yes. We're…" I let my words trail off as I sipped my cocoa.

"Dating? Genus? Living together?"

The drink warmed my insides and gave me back a shot of my normal self. "Yes," I stated simply, since all three were true.

Ash coughed as he choked on his coffee. "What? I was kidding about the living together!"

His mug hit the table with a loud clunk, coffee spilling over the rim and pooling onto the surface.

"You better clean that shit up."

I jumped at the growl from the other side of the room.

Turning in my chair, my gaze landed on a guy who looked like he just rolled out of bed. My eyes nearly popped out of my head when I realized all he wore was a pair of low-slung boxers. I could only see his back, brown hair, and the start of a tattoo on his right hip, but I was pretty sure if he turned around, I would drool.

"Put some pants on before you scar my sister for life."

No way. Turn around first. I might have boyfriends, but I wasn't dead, yet.

He turned, and I sent a little thank-you to the universe. The tat I spotted the start of swirled from his hip, across his chest, and ended on his right pec. The blue and white whorls spread chaotically over his chest, covering most of it. The light glinted off a gold hoop in one ear. His eyes speared me with a distrustful glare. I wouldn't call him model or celebrity gorgeous, but he was plenty of eye candy for me, even when his whole being screamed stay away.

"Uh-huh. Sister. Thought you were an only child? I've met your dad. I know when your mom died. She claims to be your sister, and you just believe it?" He shook his head. "How stupid can you be?" He crossed the room in a few long strides and got down into my face. "Take whatever con you're running, sweetheart, and get the fuck out."

Okay, he might be cute, but I'd had enough of being the prey tonight.

"Make me, asshole," I growled back.

He snorted a laugh and headed toward the sink. "Yep. She's a Phoenix."

Without another word, he started rinsing the dishes and loading them into the dishwasher.

I blinked, trying to adjust to the sudden change in attitude. I looked at Ash to find him shaking his head again.

"I'd tell you Zephyr doesn't mean to be an asshole, but I'd be lying. He doesn't trust easily, and he has his reasons for it." Ash reached for the roll of paper towels on the table and cleaned up the spilled coffee. "Back to you living with Kuriharas."

The thinly veiled anger in his tone confused me. The change in his attitude was hard to wrap my brain around. The late hour didn't help. I shrugged. "Some stuff happened at the dorms, and Souta's folks didn't want me going back, so they let me stay with them."

"And you and Souta?" He sat back down and aimed the now wet wad of paper towels toward the trash can, where it bounced off the side and fell to the floor with a plop.

A growl came from Zephyr as he walked over and threw it away.

"We're dating. And Genus."

A knock interrupted whatever Ash wanted to say next.

Zephyr headed for the door since he was closest. I heard his growl even in the kitchen. "You must be here for the sister."

Souta flew around the corner, hair mused, eyes darting everywhere until they landed on me sitting at the table, calmly drinking my cocoa. He dashed across the kitchen, and before I could brace myself, he lifted me from the chair, pulled me tight against him, and spun.

"Fuck, fuck, fuck. Thank the elements you're okay." He tucked his head into the crook of my shoulder and neck. "Don't you ever do that to me again. Fuck. I'm sorry, okay. We'll work things out, but fuck, don't walk away from me like that."

I wrapped my arms around his neck, knowing he needed reassurance.

"Ahem." The throat clearing got Souta's attention, and his head jerked up.

His grip on me tightened as he lowered me back to the floor, eyes shooting daggers at Ash.

"Souta." I ran a hand down his cheek to get his attention. His gaze shifted to meet mine, face and smile softening. "It's okay, we're working things out."

His gaze hardened, and he shot a glare over my shoulder to Ash. "You hurt my girl, I'll kick your fucking ass," Souta growled.

I rolled my eyes and tried to hold back a laugh. The alpha male he hid behind an easy-going mask amused me so much.

"I could say the same," Ash replied evenly. "That's my little sister you're clutching there. And let's talk about the fact she's living with you. And dating you." His tone hardened the more he talked.

Whoa, he'd gone from zero to big brother in nothing flat. I glanced back over my shoulder to find Ash with his arms crossed over his chest and a scowl on his face.

Okay.

"I don't think you have the right to call her that given how you've treated her." Souta's grip tightened again, and I squirmed to alleviate the discomfort. A stinging slap delivered to my ass told me to hold still.

Ash growled. "You did not just hit my little sister."

Okay, time to diffuse the situation. "Stop, you two. It's too late for this alpha bullshit, and I'm tired."

My hand shot out to stop Ash's advance across the kitchen while focusing my attention on the pissed off Asian holding me.

"Souta, Ash's behavior, and anything else, is between me and him. Period. I appreciate your concern, but I don't need rescuing." I swiveled my attention to my brother. "Ditto to you. He didn't mean anything by it. He'd never hurt me intentionally."

Ash didn't seem inclined to let it drop. "I don't fucking care. No one hits you. Period."

The tension thrumming through Ash's body was practically visible.

I tapped Souta's arm, and he released me, reluctance in every movement. Deliberately, I crossed the short distance between Ash and me, threw my arms around his tense frame, and hugged him briefly. After our tumultuous start, I don't know what made me do it, but it felt right.

"I'm not some shrinking wallflower, violet damsel

in distress." I spoke quietly but made sure to put strength in my words. "If something like that were happening, I would tell you. After I walked away and dealt with it. I've been taking care of myself a long time, brother. No one is going to treat me badly." My words finally seemed to hit home, and I watched him visibly relax.

"All right." His gaze darted to Souta before coming back to me. "My apology doesn't make up for what an ass I was. What happened with our folks doesn't have a damn thing to do with us. Don't be a stranger, okay? I want to get to know my little sister."

I nodded and stepped back to Souta, who wrapped an arm around me again.

"Ready?" His voice still held too much irritation for me, but I was too tired to address it tonight.

I let him turn me and lead me out to the car, my thoughts flicking back to what sent me here in the first place. I'd been utterly ridiculous, overreacting to what surely must have been normal street noises.

The drive home was quiet. I spent most of it wishing the next day was a Monday, or a Tuesday. Any day but the weekend.

Moments after we returned to Souta's house, I fell into bed, and sleep hit me hard.

EIGHTEEN

The sun coming through the window woke me the next morning moments before my guest bedroom door burst open, and the boys came barreling through.

In just lace panties and a tank, I clutched the sheet around me, only about half sure any one of them wouldn't yank it off.

"What the heck were you thinking?"

"You promised we'd talk."

"I don't like how late it was."

"Why would you do this to us?"

"How the hell did you end up with your brother?"

They talked a mile a minute, questions and worries flying furiously around me. I couldn't keep track of what they said or asked, but their fear, worry, and anger were so palpable it thickened the air in the room.

They needed to slow the hell down.

"Stop!" I barked the word. The boys froze, their gazes firmly settled on me, though their faces still held too much tension.

Fuck I was no good at this emotional shit. Wasn't that obvious from the last few weeks? I'd started to think I wasn't built for the whole family thing. Maybe that was why The Mother left me alone in the world so young.

Brooks' head tilted as I met his sympathetic gaze. He stepped closer, then sat on the edge of the bed when I didn't stop him. Though I wanted to, I didn't reach for him.

"Forgive us, beautiful." His soft voice washed over me, soothing as always. It invited me to lean into him, to give up my problems, worries, and fears and let him help make me stronger.

I blinked several times as those thoughts ran through me, not knowing when, but I'd come to think of Brooks as my pillar. He gave me strength when I needed it.

"We're as new to this as you are." Hesitantly, I slid my hand over the cool comforter to settle atop his.

"Souta texted us when you ran out at dinner and didn't respond when he tried to reach you. We all worried terribly. We care about you a great deal. I hope you know that."

I remembered seeing the texts when I'd called Souta from Ash's house, but they hadn't registered because I'd been too worried about my imaginary stalker. When he flipped his hand over, I twined our fingers together. Closing my eyes, I drew in a deep breath, felt our connection settle, and our elements sing to each other. I often wondered if others felt the things I did or if it was all in my head?

When I opened my eyes, JJ's furrowed brows darkened his golden eyes.

A pat to the bed on my other side had him close the distance in a millisecond.

"Why did you leave here like that?" JJ asked as he settled next to me and ran a hand down my cheek.

From the corner of my eye, Souta stood stiffly with his arms crossed, dark eyes flat, sleep pants riding low on his hips and revealing a hint of the elastic waistband of his underwear.

Drool.

No. Focus.

"I needed a moment to myself and only intended to walk around the block. But I wasn't paying much attention and didn't realize how long I was out, or that my ringer was silenced. I'm sorry for worrying you." My focus was on Souta as I answered JJ and apologized, hoping he'd get the message and let things drop until we could talk alone.

Souta shook out his limbs as if to force the tension away then bounded over to the bed. My message received, he was all smiles again as he leapt on the bed, using my knees as a prop to look up at me.

JJ set his arm behind my back to lean against me. "What's this about your brother?"

"I got a little freaked out when I realized nothing looked familiar." I shrugged, not really sure I could explain it since I didn't totally understand it myself. "He came to get me since I was lost. We talked. Things are better between us."

Brooks and JJ seemed to accept my words, but Souta narrowed his eyes at me.

"Now, get out of here." After untangling our hands, I shooed them. "I need to put pants on."

Souta's eyes lit up. "You're just in underwear?" He waggled his eyebrows, and I couldn't stop the laugh that escaped. "Are they black lace? No, wait, red lace." His eyes widened. "Even better red and black lace?"

When he made as if to try to remove the

comforter, I swatted his hand and laughed. "You'll have to wonder. Now out." Pointing at the door, I speared them all with a stern look.

Brooks and JJ dragged a reluctant Souta out the door, and I was left in blessed silence. Thankful for the moment alone, I slipped from the bed and knelt on the floor to draw my suitcase from under the bed. Pulling out jeans and a long-sleeved tee, I tried not to let the familiar clench of my stomach bother me as I dressed.

It only took a few moments to run a brush through my hair and another over my teeth, before I headed downstairs toward the sound of boys trying to talk Chris, the cook, into making chocolate chip pancakes.

In the kitchen, I settled onto a stool next to JJ, flopping forward onto the counter. A glass of ice water appeared in front of me, so I sat back up and downed it in one go. Ice water was far more effective in waking me up than caffeine.

Souta plopped onto the stool next to me, then pulled my stool over with one hand and worked a finger through a belt loop at my back.

JJ raised an eyebrow and reached out to pull me back toward him.

Souta growled. Actually growled.

JJ pulled his arm away, palm up, and I rolled my eyes at their antics.

The smells of a mouth-watering breakfast filled the air. A stack of pancakes, sans chocolate chips, appeared on the counter with a small pitcher of syrup. A large pitcher of orange juice, a platter with bacon, and another filled with scrambled eggs quickly followed. The boys dove in like, well, teenage boys.

"Thanks, Chris." I waved a hand at the incredible spread before us and smiled at him. "It looks delicious."

He nodded and turned away, but I didn't miss the grin that lit his face.

Souta pushed a plate in front of me.

Snatching a fork, I dug in, moaning as the perfect, fluffy pancakes hit my mouth.

"Brooks, she's doing it again. Make her stop," Souta whined next to me.

I ignored him and bit into perfectly crisp bacon and moaned again.

"Screw that. I fucking love hearing her enjoy food." When I glanced in JJ's direction, he waggled his eyebrows at me.

Brooks leaned past JJ to catch my gaze, his eyes sparkling with laughter. "Beautiful, could you kindly spare us all the painful erections that come with you loudly enjoying your food?"

Chris snorted as he cleared the pots and pans from the stove.

"I could, but what fun would that be?" Saucily, I took another bite, making sure to moan with exaggeration.

Souta growled this time and shifted closer.

The other two were also laser-focused on me.

Enjoying my torture of them a bit, I did it again.

Souta leaned in and pressed a kiss to my neck. His breath ghosted over my ear, warm and soft. "Hot stuff, if you don't behave so we can eat breakfast, I'll have to spank you later."

A pleasurable shiver ran down my spine. Since he asked so nicely, I decided enough was enough, quit moaning, but continued to dig into breakfast.

Twenty minutes later, with breakfast annihilated, we left the kitchen and made our way into our usual room. We settled onto the couches to argue over how we'd spend the rest of our day.

Curled up in a corner of the couch, Souta startled a squeak out of me when he picked me up and settled me into his lap.

"Cut it out." I shoved at his arm wrapped around

me. Sitting in someone's lap gave me the sensation of being five-years-old, and I wasn't a fan.

The arm tightened. "You're sitting here."

The steel in Souta's voice made me still my attempts to sit on my own. I uncurled, sitting stiffly on Souta's legs, hands resting on his arm. After my disappearing act last night, I didn't feel comfortable pushing him away.

Brooks rose from his seat and circled to the back of our couch. He leaned down, whispering so quietly in Souta's ear I couldn't hear.

Souta huffed as he unwrapped his arm from me.

I slid off his lap and settled in next to him, grateful to be back on the couch.

We vegged out to a couple movies before Brooks' phone chimed. He checked it and frowned. "I need to go. Family stuff." The annoyance dripped from his words.

Family stuff seemed to crop up more and more lately, and he appeared increasingly annoyed.

He unfolded himself from the chair, patted JJ's shoulder, and gave Souta and me quick kisses before heading out the door. With his exit, my grace period was expiring quickly.

When JJ rose a bare fifteen minutes later, I knew it would soon be time to face the music.

"I'm gonna take off, too. I've got a sculpture calling my name." He kissed me, hard and fast, and headed out.

With JJ and Brooks gone, I knew hiding in my room wouldn't delay the talk we should have had last night, so I didn't bother to try.

When Souta rose, I followed him up to his room.

The silence weighed heavy between us, and I wiped my palms on my jeans.

In his room, I curled into one of the chairs and waited for the questions, unsure if he would blow a fuse first. For all of his flirty, hyper, happy demeanor there were a lot more facets to Souta than most thought.

Souta sank onto his bed, sitting stiffly on the side, hands curling around the edge of the mattress, and head hanging to stare at the floor. His shoulders rose and fell as he breathed in a slow, steady rhythm.

"Why—" He bit off the angry word, took another breath in, still focusing on the floor instead of me. "Why would you call him?" He spat the word him out like a slur. I opened my mouth to respond, but Souta was quicker. "No, wait. Let's back up. What happened?" His eyes finally raised to meet mine.

"It was stupid, honestly." Since I hadn't seen anyone or anything to be concerned about, I truly believed I overreacted. "It was dark, and I kept hearing these sounds." I waved away the concern on his face. "Just leaves and ordinary night noises, I'm sure, but between realizing I didn't recognize the area and the dark, I freaked a little."

Souta shook his head and gave me a stern look full of disbelief. "Not good enough, hot stuff."

"I thought I heard someone following me, okay?" Sighing, I pulled my legs up and wrapped my arms around them. I didn't want to tell him that since it made me look ridiculous. "I never saw anyone, or even anything, to indicate anyone was there, it was just my head being stupid."

Souta stood abruptly and paced toward the door, running a hand through his hair. "So, you got scared, and instead of calling me or JJ or Brooks, or even my folks, or—fucking hell—Maybelle, you call that asshole?" He spun, brow creased but nostrils flaring. "Why? I don't understand. Why him over everyone else? Over me?"

Dread was heavy inside me, I didn't fully understand it myself, only parts of the why. "You only saw him the once at Michael's—Dad's. I saw him a couple times after that." Fury flew across his features at my words, but I barreled ahead before he could interrupt. "That first day was the worst, and he wasn't pleasant for the second, but Ash's anger never felt directed at me. I was a convenient target."

His scowl told me I wasn't making sense to him, but I kept trying. "The second time I saw him at Michael—Dad's—he walked in on us looking at some old photos of my mom. Turned out he'd heard stories about her and shared them with me. After, it seemed like something shifted, softened?" Rubbing my hands over my knees, I wasn't able to explain it better.

"So, when I freaked out, yeah, I thought of you first, but I was still upset and not ready to talk to you. Then, I found his number in my phone. I'd forgotten Michael—Dad—put it in there, and somehow, it just made sense at that moment to call him." I met the hot frustration in his brown eyes and added, "Honestly, Souta, I'm glad I did. We talked while we waited for you. Nothing serious, but he did apologize, and afterward, things felt easier. Like we were finally bonding or some shit."

"He rejected you, for fuck's sake, without even trying to get to know you." Souta's volume escalated. "But now everything's fine because you heard a few stories, and he didn't leave you on the street in the dead of night?" He lowered his voice as if realizing how loud he'd gotten.

Clearly, neither of us wanted his folks hearing this.

As his words sank in, they fueled my irritation. He wasn't even trying to understand. My gaze took him in, noting the tension in the way he stood, slightly hunched posture and the clenched fists. Why was this bothering him so damn much?

"Doing one decent thing doesn't negate his treatment of you, Sera! You shouldn't have anything to do with him!"

"Just like that, huh?" My voice came out even and level, but anger burned through me.

The pungent aroma of burning cloth reached my nose, and I glanced down at my hands, tightly gripping the arms of the chair, to find smoke curling from under them.

Removing my hands, I clutched them in my lap and returned my attention to Souta. "Just turn my back on my family."

"We're your family! You don't need any other family!" His vehemence echoed around the room, and he stepped forward but stopped when I stood abruptly.

He must have seen his own anger reflected on my face.

"You don't get it. None of you do. How could

you? How could you possibly understand the yearning, the need for family? To have somewhere to belong, for people who will accept and love you unconditionally? How could you know what it's like when you all sit here with your perfect families, doting parents and grandparents?" My arm swung out to encompass the whole of his room and house. "You know where you came from, can probably trace your line back a few generations at least, but you don't need to."

Gulping for air, I rushed on, "You know they existed. People who helped shape you by shaping the ones before you. You don't know what it feels like on Family Day at school to watch everyone, literally every single fucking person around you, with their families and wish you had someone, anyone, there so you wouldn't have to stand in a corner hiding from the pitying glances of your schoolmates and their families! To spend every holiday with someone else's perfect family, wishing you had one."

My vision blurred, and tears ran down cheeks. "For the first time, I have a chance for a real family, and you want me to walk away because we had a rough start?" My voice cracked. I didn't care anymore about his why, this hurt too much.

"So, we're not a real family?" He stepped away,

hurt and anger chasing across his features, and stormed back toward his bed, his words spitting out like sharp daggers. "Our Genus, what you have with me, with the others, isn't real enough for you?"

His words felt like a physical slap. He knew how I felt about them, about him, was different. Didn't he? My heart hurt as I stared at this flushed, angry stranger. The Genus may have brought us together, but was I expected to actually choose between one almost family and another? I couldn't do this anymore.

Squaring my shoulders, I strode toward the door. "I can't be who you want me to be, I can't give up on a father and brother I just found." Pausing with my hand on the knob, I looked back over my shoulder at him. He stood by his bed, arms crossed over his chest. "I'm sorry."

"Yeah, sure. Just walk away like always." His tone was so cold a shiver ran down my spine. "Better to have no one than feel something, right?"

With that final spear to my heart, I turned and left, not stopping even as I walked through the door and off the grounds.

If this was what it was like to risk your heart, I didn't know if I wanted any part of it.

NINETEEN

I walked without paying attention to where my feet led me. My steps stumbled, uneven, over the smooth ground. My thoughts spun, circling around the boys, their families, Michael, and Ash. A tornado of thoughts, feelings, and questions with no answers whirled too fast to nail down any one individual item.

It overwhelmed me, nausea rising as my knees weakened. As I stumbled again, I thrust a handout to catch myself, and rough, sharp bark bit into my palm with little notice by me.

"Sera!"

I wanted to go back. Back to when things were simple. When the only person I needed to worry about was me—no boys, no family, just me. Things didn't hurt so much then. Things didn't swirl in a muddled confusion. I didn't know how to do this. How to balance everything, how to be the person everyone wanted. Especially when they all wanted something different: a daughter, a sister, a girlfriend, and a lover.

"Sera!"

I closed my eyes and took a deep breath. Freaking out wouldn't solve anything. I needed to pull myself together. *Running wouldn't either,* a tiny voice inside my head mocked me. It was true, but I couldn't face Souta right now. *We're not real enough for you?* Souta's words reared up and slapped me again.

A push against the rough bark had me stumble forward a couple steps.

Muscular arms wrapped around me, catching me before my knees hit the dirt. For a moment, the merest slip of a half a second, I thought Brooks somehow caught me.

Then, looking up derailed my hope.

Dane.

What? My brain stuttered.

"Are you okay?" His forehead creasing as he held me up.

He didn't clutch me to him like Souta. He didn't hold me with care and a reassuring stroke of his fingers like Brooks. He didn't pull me in to rest against him like JJ. I would have expected any one of those things, given his history.

Instead, he moved his hands from my waist and gripped my arms lightly but firm enough to ensure I wouldn't fall.

Once, I would have pulled out of his grip, uncomfortable with the touch of someone I hardly knew and pissed he would try to make a move.

Now, his grip made me realize how much I'd come to love the ways my boys touched me, held me. Loved the way each felt unique but important. Dane's touch didn't reassure me or give me strength, but it also didn't upset me. It simply existed, holding on until my strength returned, then letting go quickly and easily.

"Sera?" The obvious concern in his voice jerked me out of my own head.

I met his concerned blue gaze and mentally shook myself.

"I... what?" It dawned on me I didn't know what he wanted.

Had he been talking? Asking me something?

"Are you okay?" He waved a hand toward the footpath I somehow failed to register. "You nearly walked in front of a bike."

"I… I…" I shook my head.

No, I wasn't okay. Far from it, but I wasn't about to dump on Dane. What the hell was he doing here, anyway? We met here the one time. Did he live nearby? And why was he acting… nice? Shouldn't he be taking this opportunity to make a move on me?

"You don't look good. Should I call Souta?" He stepped forward again, hand closing around my forearm as he frowned.

"Get your hands off my girlfriend, Hicks!"

My head jerked around at the familiar, commanding tone.

Souta strode toward us, sunlight glinting off his dark-brown locks and lighting up the tension on his face.

Dane smirked, his free hand suddenly finding my waist as he yanked me against him. "Maybe she likes my hands on her, Sue. After all, you've only got two, and they always seem a little busy with that cute blond of yours."

The fuck? For element's sake.

With a growl, Souta lunged at Dane.

I rolled my eyes and heated my arm faster than ever before.

Dane released me with a yelp but stood his ground as Souta slammed a fist into his gut. Huffing out a breath, Dane's hand went to his stomach, but he didn't retaliate.

Damn good thing, too, or I might have let Souta get a few more punches in for that asshole move of Dane's.

"Cut it the fuck out, Souta!" I hollered as I grabbed his arm when he drew back for another punch.

Spinning on his heel, all grace even this pissed off, his dark eyes flashed as they landed on me hurt, obliterating the anger for a second before being buried again.

Still upset, I didn't bother to hide my hurt as I straightened and squared my shoulders. "Why are you here, Souta?"

"I'm not about to let you run the fuck away, again."

A mild breeze blew the short, red strands of my hair into disarray, odd since none existed a moment ago. It pinged the edges of my brain, trying to tickle something out, but I ignored it.

"I'm not running away." It took effort to keep my voice even and calm, the irritation at him burning through me. "I needed a few minutes alone. That's all. I just— I'm not used to all of this, and I don't—"

I cut off abruptly as Souta shook his head, arms

crossed over his chest.

My eyes burned at the way he closed himself off, but I needed to make him understand. "Dammit, I've been alone for eighteen years. I don't know how to do all this!" My voice rose as my stomach cramped. "I just needed a little alone time, for fuck's sake!"

"And you couldn't do that at home?"

"No! I couldn't!" Dammit, why wouldn't he listen? Why wasn't he understanding? A sinking feeling started in my gut, but I refused to crumble, heart wrapped up tight, in hopes of avoiding more pain. "It's not like I can lock doors there if I need to be on my own for a bit. It's not my home!"

Souta's gaze darted between Dane and me, and his eyes widened a fraction. For a heartbeat, I watched as he folded in on himself, as his face distorted in heartache. He wiped it away so quickly I almost thought I imagined it.

"Not your—" He shook his head and glared at Dane. "So, instead of bringing it up, or fucking asking us not to disturb you, you walk out of our house and right into some other guy's arms?" His voice hardened as he spoke, eyes glinting in the light before he blinked. He glared at Dane briefly before turning to me. I was a little surprised Dane still stood there. "How long?"

What was he asking? I frowned, tilting my head. "How long what?"

"How long, Sera! How long has this been going on, since it's been more than a fucking school project?" Souta jabbed a finger in Dane's direction as his volume rose. "We said we didn't mind sharing you, but we meant with each other! Me. JJ. Brooks! Period! Not some random guy! And you... You're going behind our fucking backs!"

I glanced around, surprised to find ourselves far enough away that the one woman who watched us was scurrying away as fast as she could. It hit me then, what he was saying.

"You think I'm"—my mouth gaped, throat so tight I couldn't even get the word out—"with Dane?"

Dane heaved a sigh, the smirk long ago fallen from his face as he watched us. Meeting my eyes, I read the apology in his gaze for causing this fight, for making a scene, but he wasn't to blame. If blame lay anywhere, it was with me. "It hasn't been like that, Sue. Matter of fact—"

"Shut up!" Souta shouted, cutting him off. "Just shut up! You're not taking her from us! You're not going wreck our Genus!"

The vehemence in his voice made me step back. Moments before I left, he was accusing me of not believing we were a real family, and now, he was pissed because he thought someone was trying to break us up? I couldn't make heads or tails of any of this.

A bruising grip closed around my upper arms, yanking me backward.

My feet stumbled over the rocks and grass, nearly sending me to my ass.

Twisting, I tried to catch a glance of whoever dragged me.

When I finally caught a glimpse of him, my heart raced, and I gasped. It was that guy I'd seen at school, the *harmless* nutcase.

I kicked at the guy, twisting and pulling as I screamed, "Souta!"

He growled, grip tightening on my arms, and continued jerking me farther from the open area.

Not today, asshole! I heated my arms as quickly as I could, hoping to burn his hands. He didn't flinch, and the smell of burning flesh never arose.

What by all the elements is happening? How was he not hurt?

The guy, what the fuck was his name again, hissed as he yanked me closer. "Stop that! I'm trying to help you!"

Was the fucker delusional? Kicking, pulling, and

twisting, I fought against his grip.

A strong breeze rushed at me, and my head jerked up. Souta stood, face twisted in a scowl, hand thrust out. Next to him, Dane's scowl matched Souta's.

As the breeze knocked into us, the guy stumbled but didn't release me. Regaining his balance, he pulled me until I came up flush against him, face to face. In a tone too low for anyone else to hear, he hissed in my ear, "I know that necklace. That's the symbol of Embers."

What the fuck was he talking about? My necklace? I always wore it, though I didn't think about it much anymore. Putting it out of my mind and not giving up, I lunged forward, determined to bite the guy, anything to get him to release his hold on me.

"Hands off, asshole!" Souta screamed behind me.

The stiff gust of wind rushing by moments later knocked me to my knees and sent my captor stumbling back.

Souta and Dane rushed to my side.

As the guy found his footing again, I rose with the help of Souta's outstretched hand.

Standing in front of us, Dane crossed his arms and held up the hand clutching his phone. "Come any closer, and I call the Lex," he spat out.

The guy stopped, eyes fixated on me. It felt, for a moment, as if he was trying to send me a message, to reach out and invade my mind.

A chill ran down my spine, and I leaned into Souta's comfort as he wrapped an arm around my waist.

"You're making a mistake," he stated as though he knew all the facts.

The guy was nuts.

"You made the mistake, Chester." Souta's arm tightened his hold as he spoke. "When you tried to take Sera from me."

Chester shrugged. "We'll see." His creepy gaze never left me. "You don't belong with them. But you'll know that soon enough." He tilted his head at me, as though tipping a cap. "See you soon, my dear."

He shot me a cocky smirk and raced away through the trees.

Clenching my hands in Souta's shirt, I drew in a deep breath to still my shaking. When that didn't help, I buried my face against his chest.

"Thank you." My muffled words were answered with a huff.

Chester trying to drag me away took only moments, but it felt as though it stretched for so much longer. The fear of not being able to get away from him distorted my sense of time.

"Don't thank me. I had nothing to do with it." Souta's fingers found my chin, lifting it so I met his eyes. I expected humor or his usual sparkle. Instead, the only sparkle I found was a hard, angry glint. "Apparently, you need to thank your other boyfriend."

"Someone tried to kidnap me, and you want to go back to this?" What, by all the elements, was his fucking problem? I pulled out of his embrace. "Nothing is going on!"

Dane shifted to stand off to our side. He held his hands up in surrender, trying to appease my pissed off, irrational boyfriend. "I can't do anything that strong."

"Oh, yeah?" Souta faced him.

Wanting, or rather hoping, to diffuse the situation, I settled my hand on Souta's arm.

He shrugged off my touch. "I sure as hell didn't send that gust of wind. I can't produce anything that strong yet, either. But you were right there, hand out, just as he was knocked off his feet by wind. Tell me again how you didn't do anything, Dane."

"I never said I didn't do anything." Hands still held up, Dane's tone was carefully measured as if he recognized the hair-trigger Souta seemed to be standing on. "I did send a gust, but I'm serious about the strength. I've never even knocked over an empty can before."

Dane grimaced as if the admission pained him, which it likely did. He couldn't be very strong if he couldn't knock over an empty can. I'd seen Souta knock over a small pyramid of them once in training.

"You don't fool me for a second." Spit and anger no longer laced Souta's voice, but now, it sounded flat.

What he was thinking or feeling? I wished I knew what to do right now. My gaze slid back and forth between them, Dane's expression still concerned while Souta's remained stoic. My vision blurred as my mind curled in on itself.

Between the fight about family, the accusations from Souta, and the crazy guy trying to drag me off, it was too much. My ears rang and drowned out their argument as a wave of cold washed over me. Tears streaked down my cheeks, but they didn't stop me from seeing Souta's whole focus was only on Dane.

The shakes returned, and my knees wobbled. I was moments from collapsing.

With a last look at Souta, who still argued with a placating Dane, I turned and ran.

TWENTY

My feet automatically headed in the direction of Souta's house, but I couldn't go back there. Not now. A part of me wanted to call Brooks or JJ.

Reaching in my pocket, I dug out my phone, then stared at Brooks' number.

Did he share Souta's feelings? What about JJ? Did they all think I took our relationship, our Genus so lightly? How could I talk to them about us when I couldn't even figure out me? As much as it hurt, I knew I still needed time away, so I didn't continue to act rashly and blow the first good thing to ever come my way.

The phone shook in my hand. The shaking was

getting worse, and it was harder to lift my feet. I stumbled, tripping over nothing. When I glanced around, the houses were all familiar. I was nearing Souta's.

Not stopping, I tucked my head and speed-walked past it. Around the corner and out of sight, my knees finally gave out. Crashing to a stop, I barely caught myself with my hands before I face-planted into the pavement.

My phone went tumbling down the sidewalk. I scrambled after it and prayed it still worked. Flipping it over, I breathed a sigh of relief when I saw the screen was only scratched.

Barely holding it together, I couldn't get up and keep walking. I couldn't help the shiver of fear at the thought of Chester finding me now. Flipping through my contacts, I debated who to call. May? No, she'd told me she'd be hard to reach for the next few months, so no guarantees. Ash entered my mind, but with Souta's reaction combined with us just starting to figure things out as siblings, asking him to deal with all this or listen while I bitched about my boyfriends might be pushing the boundaries.

Michael. Dad. His number was right there. While I wouldn't want to share what was going on, he told me to call him anytime. Well, text him, but same thing. I didn't let myself second-guess the choice and popped open a text message.

Sera: Hi, Dad.

The word, Dad, made me grin through my tears as I typed it. Calling him Dad was getting easier.

Sera: Are you home or on duty? Can I call you?

His response came almost immediately

Michael: I'm home, sweetheart. You can call. Everything okay?

No. Everything wasn't okay. Far from it, but I didn't want to get into it in text. Instead, I hit call.

He picked up before the first ring ended. "Hi, sweetie."

A strange sensation of love filtered through his words, and my voice cracked hearing it. "Hi, Dad."

"Sera, what's wrong?"

I ran a hand over my face to wipe away the tears. "Can you come get me? I'm around the corner from Souta's." I glanced at the street sign above me to give him the exact location. "Seneca and Vine."

"I'll be there in a couple minutes. Don't move." He hung up, and the floodgates opened.

He hadn't even questioned why I wanted him to come. Hadn't wondered why I didn't just go to

Souta's. I asked him to come, and he was coming. No questions, no conditions.

Was this what they meant by unconditional love? Was this what family was meant to be? I pulled my legs up, wrapped my arms around my knees, and buried my face in them as I cried.

By the time the rumble of a car pulled up beside me and stopped, I'd cried myself out and reached numb. I lifted my head as Dad got out and circled around the car.

From the way his eyes widened, I must have looked a mess, tears obvious on my face.

He knelt beside me and wrapped strong arms around me in a comforting embrace. "Come on. Let's get you home."

He pulled me closer, somehow managing to pick me up as he stood. I curled into him, taking the comfort he offered.

Home. I didn't know where that was anymore. Did I still have a home with the boys? And if they were my home, why had I always felt like a guest at Souta's?

Dad tucked me into his car, and we took off.

The ride wasn't long enough for me to do more than wonder how things ended between Souta and Dane.

Calmer and still feeling numb, I exited the car and headed toward the house. Michael followed. I walked in the front door but halted on the other side. I needed a bed and a nap and to let myself fall apart, but I didn't know where to go.

The hand that landed on my shoulder caused me to startle.

"Follow me." Dad smiled and jerked his head toward the stairs, and we started up. "This might have been a little presumptuous, and honestly, don't feel like you can't tell us you hate it." He stopped at a door at the top of the stairs, placing a hand on the knob. "We tried to decorate it in a fashion we thought you'd like, but I'm used to teenage boys, not girls, so…"

His shrug was apologetic as I stared blankly at him.

"Kelly and I were hoping to tell you, or ask you, a little differently, but you look about ten seconds from collapsing." He opened the door and gave a small flourish for me to enter.

As I stepped in, my eyes barely took in the space. Too tired and wiped out to take a good look, I made my way to the white daybed loaded with pillows, none of the frilly variety, and covered in a black-and-red patterned quilt. Without another thought, I collapsed onto the bed, grabbing one of the pillows decorated with flames and curled around it.

"Sera, honey." Dad brushed a hand over my hair. Even through my numb haze, I marveled at how it felt to have someone, a parent, comfort me. "Will you tell me what's going on?"

Unable to answer, I shook my head.

I didn't want to talk.

Didn't want to think.

Didn't want to feel.

Just wanted to drift.

"Okay, well, Kelly and I planned to ask you to come to stay with us, so don't feel like you have a time limit here or anything. This is your room now." He pressed a kiss to my head and rose.

As he left, I heard him say, "Ash. Your sister's here…"

If he said anything else, it was lost as he closed the door and walked down the hall, and I drifted to sleep.

I didn't sleep long, about forty-five minutes according to my phone. My eyes caught the waiting text. Throat tightening, I swallowed hard, unable to face him yet, but not responding would be cruel.

Souta: Sera! Where are you?
Sera: I'm okay.

My fingers hesitated with my mind stumbling to find the words. After staring at the phone for a full two minutes, I deleted the whole thing and started again.

Sera: I'm at my dad's. I need time, please.

Truthful was the best I could do and be. I wasn't okay, far from it, and I needed to stop telling them that I was. Souta would respond right away, but I couldn't do this right now. Guilt swamped me as I shut off my phone.

Tossing my phone onto the nightstand, I finally took the time to look around. In addition to the bed, there was a dresser and nightstand in white. The room held little else, giving me the impression of a blank canvas. Soft, dove-gray walls and matching carpet helped the white furniture blend in. It was oddly soothing, and I loved how the beautiful red and black patchwork quilt stood out.

My gaze caught again on my phone, silent on the nightstand.

How had I managed to screw up so badly? Used to being alone, I knew I had a lot to learn. Suddenly finding myself surrounded by people who wanted to be close to me left me stumbling around blind. I thought we were doing okay at first. We talked. We connected. Then, we stopped talking. *I* stopped talking. And the misunderstandings began.

What had I done, or not done, to leave Souta with those feelings?

Had the Mother made a mistake, putting me with them? Did the Mother make mistakes? No, this was on me. If we fell apart, I would be the one to blame. Unable to be who they expected me to be, I wanted to curl up on the bed as the realization hit me. Just forget the world, hide away from everything.

The darkness was a weight trying to descend around me. It wasn't me. It would never be me. So, I refused to let it take hold. I'd screwed up, true. Now, I had to figure out who I was, how I felt, and what to do about it.

A soft knock on the door preceded a head peeking in. "I just wanted to check on you." Kelly smiled as she stepped in. "Your dad didn't say much about what's going on. Do you need to talk?"

She sat on the bed next to me, but with a distance I felt comfortable with. She pushed her dark hair behind her ear as she turned to face me.

I didn't want to hurt her feelings but...

"I'm sorry." I shook my head. "I don't feel comfortable telling you."

Her smile didn't dim. "No worries. I'd be surprised if you did. Feel up to coming downstairs, maybe joining us for a light bite?"

Of course, my stomach chose that moment to speak up.

We both grinned as I nodded.

Neither of us spoke as we went down to the kitchen.

Dad stood at the brown and black granite counter of the large kitchen island, sunlight from a large picture window behind him streaming in and bouncing off the stainless-steel appliances.

He glanced over his shoulder as we entered.

Kelly gestured to the round, ashy brown table and chairs. "Let's eat."

Pulling out one of the chairs next to her, I sat.

"Hey. Did you let your boys know where you are?" he asked.

I nodded, hoping he wouldn't probe any further.

He grabbed a couple things off the counter and joined us at the table. When I noticed the egg salad sandwiches and fruit, I choked back a sob. Souta made the same for our date.

The hurt must have shown because Kelly's hand squeezed my shoulder. "Hey, I'm sure it will be okay, whatever it is."

Needing a minute to collect myself, I scrubbed my hands over my face, stood, and headed over to the glass-fronted, wood cabinets. If I remembered correctly, the one to the left of the sink held the glasses. Opening the cabinet door, I took a few deep breaths before grabbing a glass and pouring myself some ice water.

As I sat back down, Dad and Kelly grinned at each other, then me. "What?"

"It's nice to see you comfortable here." Dad's words hit me like bricks. I'd only been here a handful of times, but after the first few times, it felt comfortable in a way it didn't at Souta's.

"Hey, Dad, where's—" Through my shocked haze, Ash's voice cut off. He sank into the last chair at the table. "Hey, sis." He nudged me with an elbow. "You all right?"

Still lost in my shock, I failed to respond.

He turned to Dad. "Any idea what's up?"

I forced myself out of my fog, to notice the concern on the faces of my family.

Wow. My family.

They were my family, and they were worried about me. Me. I didn't want to talk to Dad, but maybe Ash would get it? It felt a bit weird since we'd only barely begun to try being siblings. Still, I wasn't getting anywhere on my own.

I turned to look at Ash, my brother whose ear and advice I really needed right now. "Can we talk?"

TWENTY-ONE

Back in my room, I flopped down onto my bed, grabbed a pillow, and curled around it. Ash's brown gaze drifted around the room slowly. I still marveled at how much like the Phoenix men I looked. Though Ash wore his hair in short spikes with blond highlights, the brown locks remained the same as my natural hair color. We both had slight builds, tending toward slender without really trying, but of course, Ash was several inches taller. It hit me that I didn't know what room I'd taken. Fuck.

"Dad said they did this room up for me. I didn't take your room, did I?" I sat up, bringing the pillow with me.

Ash grinned for the first time around me. I got

the impression this happy, easy guy was closer to who he actually was. "Nah. My room is next door. This was Dad's 'office', more of a junk room than anything else. He never actually worked on anything in here. This is a good change." He sunk onto the bed, scooting back until he rested against the backboard. "Besides, I haven't lived here for a couple years now, not since my own Genus completed. Now, what's up?"

"I'm… confused, worried, scared, I don't know…" I gripped the little orange pillow tighter as my entire body tensed up.

"Hey." Ash reached out, one hand gently undoing the death grip of my fingers. "Relax. Don't worry about feelings right now. Let's start with facts, okay?"

I nodded. Facts. I could do facts.

"Good. What happened to bring you here? Dad said you seemed like something was seriously wrong."

Telling him about the fight between Souta and me wasn't the right place to start; Ash wouldn't understand unless I backtracked and told him what lead to it. I took a deep breath, and the whole damn story spilled out in fits and starts. There were moments where I had to pause to figure out how much to tell Ash. Eventually, I gave up editing things out and just told him everything. I was out of my element so far; I wouldn't be able to find my way with a clearly lit path.

He listened, just listened, while I spilled everything. And I didn't stop with the incident yesterday, or the whole thing with Dane. Once I started, I couldn't seem to contain it anymore. All my fears and worries, every feeling and thought, every little thing that twisted up inside me, that told me I wasn't good enough, everything came crashing out of me at one time.

My voice cracked. I started to go hoarse, but I needed to finish.

Finally, the words stopped, and I fell silent. No tears, no choking, no sobbing. It felt good to finally have someone who listened to me. While I could talk to Brooks, I needed someone outside of us, someone not invested in our Genus, to help me find my way through.

"Wow." Ash spoke the single word in a flat tone.

I waited for more, but he remained silent for a few minutes, taking it all in likely.

"Can I ask you something?" He shifted, spinning to face me and resting his arms on his knees. "Something kind of sensitive?" Out of words, I just nodded. "You never had any kind of family? I mean, what about holidays and summers and stuff?"

Not wanting to relive the whole affair with Tara and Mark, I sighed. "I stayed with a family from the time I was born until just before I started school. They weren't able to continue my care at that point." I shrugged. "After that May couldn't find a permanent place, so eventually, the Concilium decided to just board me at school and told her to quit trying to find permanent placement. During breaks, they shuffled me to various families."

"And you moved schools every year?" I nodded to his question, still confused as to why they chose to do it. He shook his head. "What were they thinking? You really have no idea how to—"

"—be a normal person?" I finished for him.

He lightly smacked my leg. "No, brat. It's just that there's a dynamic that develops when you've known someone for a long time, and another that develops with family. You've missed out on all that. And in the process, you never figured out how to make those connections."

He didn't know the half of it. I closed myself so tightly against any relationships I never had a hope of figuring out how to connect. Not knowing what to say, I opened my mouth, but stopped.

"Look, I don't know much about relationships

but I gotta say"—Ash leaned forward—"you gotta quit running."

"Running?" I froze in place.

Souta said something similar, but I wasn't running, was I?

"Yeah. I get the need for time to calm down or think, I do, Sera, but you don't seem to be just taking time. From what you said, you don't talk about what's bothering you or even talk at all, you shut down and run."

"I mean, kind of. We have talked some..." But he was right. Whenever I left, or locked myself away, when I emerged again or the boys followed me, we didn't talk about why.

Was he right? Was I running? And if I was, what was I running from? The boys? I didn't think so. Well, not exactly. There was so much, though, so many feelings, clashes, and just stuff. I never had to worry about anyone except myself before. Now, I felt torn apart all the time, trying to make everyone happy.

"How do you do it?" I asked.

"Do what?" Ash's brow furrowed as his head tilted to the side.

"Make everyone happy. Be who they want you to be. I can't—"

Ash cut me off with a shake of his head. "Who

278

the hell gave you that idea?" He slashed a hand through the air. "You don't."

"Don't?"

"You don't try to be what anyone wants you to be, Seraphina. You need to be you, and that's all. If they don't like you the way you are, they aren't worth your time."

"But I wanted to make them happy, and I'm so confused."

"Before you were a Genus, before you wanted to be with them, they liked you, right?"

I nodded.

"That's my point. They liked you. The person you already were. Not the person you think they want you to be. You don't need to change for them. No one should ask that of you, Dad and I included."

As his words sank in, it felt like a huge weight lifted off my shoulders. I'd been working so hard, tearing myself apart, going crazy to be what I thought everyone wanted me to be. The perfect: Ignis, sister, daughter, girlfriend, and student.

But he was telling me I didn't need to do that anymore. I didn't need to be perfect. I only needed to be me.

"I do hope, though, you didn't leave your boys hanging."

Uncomfortable, I tugged on my hair. "I told them where I was..."

Although I did turn off my phone afterward. I bit my lip and wondered if that qualified.

Ash caught the giveaway. "But?"

"I turned my phone off afterward."

Ash sighed and looked over at the dresser. "Where—"

I pointed to the nightstand before he could finish the question. He leaned over the bed and dug around in the drawer, pulling my phone out a few moments later.

As he sat back up, he held the phone out to me. "Time to stop running."

For a minute I sat there, staring at the small electronic device like a deadly snake. Then, I gave myself a mental smack and took the phone.

Turning it on made it nearly vibrate out of my hand. Notification after notification lit the screen, and my stomach churned. Missed calls and texts awaited my attention. I only caught a hint of them as they flashed on my screen. The general gist wasn't angry, though. They were worried, about me specifically.

When I looked up, Ash's gaze caught mine. "They're worried, aren't they?"

"How do you know all this?"

He was only three years older than me. Did he have a serious girlfriend or something?

He shook his head. "Whatever you're thinking, the answer is no. I had a good teacher." He grinned wide, eyes sparkling. "We call him Dad."

I grinned back at his corny joke and noticed the phone quit vibrating. For a second, I debated between calling and texting, finally deciding to send a group text since we needed to talk in person.

Sera: I'm sorry for ignoring you all. Can you come to Michael's? I think it's time we talked about some things.

Hating the sound of the text but unable to figure out how to word it better I hit send. Hope warred with fear; the boys better not think I was going to break up with them or something. Wasn't that usually what followed the 'We Need to Talk' phrase? I didn't have enough time to worry since my phone pinged a text about thirty seconds later.

Brooks: On our way, beautiful. Happy to hear from you.

The short text didn't give me any clue about how they felt. Setting the phone down, I took a deep breath and tried not to worry. This was why we needed to talk. But right now, I needed a distraction.

"Tell me what Dad was like when you were

growing up." Ash laughed as I settled back into the mounds of pillows.

"Oh, man, you've opened the floodgates." He leaned back too before he launched into a story about Dad trying to build him a treehouse.

Apparently, Dad couldn't build things or fix things, but he wouldn't admit it, so he tried, anyway. Ash learned early to call Dad's best friend, Hugh, when he tried to fix or build anything.

Ash managed to keep me distracted with Dad's antics until the doorbell rang.

When I put the pillow on the bed and started to rise, Ash stopped me with a hand on my arm. "Give me a minute? I want to talk to them first."

I nodded and promptly started picking at my nails when he got up and left. Why did he want to talk to them?

Curiosity got the better of me, and standing, I slipped out of my room to eavesdrop.

The stairs ended near the door, and the second-floor landing overlooked the foyer. Not wanting anyone to see me, I stopped short of the actual landing, at the edge of the wall, letting it hide me.

"One of you boys want to explain to me why I picked my daughter up from the side of the road looking like her world exploded?" Dad's stern tone as he addressed the boys sent a shudder through me. I hoped his barely restrained anger never had a reason to be directed at me.

Souta spoke up. "It's my fault, sir."

It wasn't his fault, though, not entirely. I was as much to blame for my unhappiness as anyone else. More so, really.

Dad growled a single word, "Explain."

It seemed unnatural to me, unlike the happy, easy man I'd begun to think of as my father.

"Dad," Ash said.

Oh, good. Maybe he'd stop this caveman conversation. Needing to catch a glimpse of my boys, I peered around the corner.

Ash's hand rested on Dad's arm as their gazes met.

Dad nodded at some unspoken cue.

The boys, though... Oh, dear.

Souta alternated between bouncing in place and trying to pace. Brooks kept pulling him back. JJ's hair looked like he'd run his hands through it several times. All of their shoulders slumped, clothes rumpled. If I could see their eyes better, would they be dull and flat?

I pulled back to hide behind the wall again.

So much stress and worry; I did this to them.

How could I be worth it to them when all I did was screw things up?

"Look," Ash said. "We don't know what happened, and that's between you and Seraphina, but she's hurting right now. There's a lot you all need to work out from the sounds of things. Know that I'll be keeping half an eye on you all. Do right by her or you'll answer to both of us. That's my little sister up there, don't forget it."

"Oh, yeah." Souta's sneer was clear in his voice. "Now, she's your little sister? What the fuck happened to 'You are not my sister. I will never accept that.'?"

"That's between me and Sera."

Souta's voice rose. "The fuck it is!"

Ash met Souta's heat with ice. "It really is."

It was time to put an end to this before Souta got going.

I stepped out from behind the wall. "Souta. Not now."

My voice was even and caught his attention quickly. His head jerked up, eyes wide as they found me.

"Sera." He spoke my name on a breath of air, and I nearly missed the single word.

He started toward the stairs but stopped. His eyes closed, and his entire body slumped. Opening his eyes, he lifted his gaze to mine, uncertainty written in every line on his face.

I hated seeing him like this, as less than his joyous self. Offering a half-smile, I opened my arms.

His face lit up as he slipped past Ash, ran up the stairs, barreled into me, and lifted me off the floor to swing me around in a tight hug. My insides lit up as I hugged him back. Only a few hours passed, but it felt like days. I missed them. It felt so good to be held by him again after thinking I might have lost them.

He set me down, and we stepped out of our embrace.

"Come on." I headed down the stairs to where the others waited.

Time to figure our shit out.

TWENTY-TWO

As we spread around the couches and chairs in the living room, a part of me wanted to curl up inside my head and hide behind the facade again. Hopefully, I shoved that cowardly bitch aside so hard she'd take years to come back. I was done trying to be a people pleaser. The boys stayed silent, waiting on me.

"First, let me apologize." Souta opened his mouth to interrupt me, but I held up a hand to hold him off. "I should never have run off, last night or today." My hand shook, and I buried it under my thigh to hide my nerves. Would they hate me for what I admitted? "Talking to Ash made me realize a couple things. The main one is that I've been running."

"From what?" JJ's brow furrowed as he frowned.

With a deep breath, I braced myself for their reaction as I admitted, "From my feelings. From my family. From you."

Silence prevailed. The words hung between us, a weight suspended by the thinnest thread. One breath would bring the whole thing crashing down. Waiting for the inevitable became painful. I sank my teeth into my bottom lip.

"Why?" The softly spoken word came from Brooks.

Now came the hard part. Understanding would be difficult, and it meant I couldn't hold anything back anymore. They knew a little about my past, but not all of it.

"I don't know how to do this." I circled the room with a finger, indicating them and me. "I've never even tried to connect to others. I don't know how to be part of anything. Not friends or being a daughter or a girlfriend or a Genus. Not anything, much less the family you all keep telling me we are. I know it's hard to understand, but it started a long time ago." I studied each of them, noticing for the first time Brooks and Souta sat in separate chairs.

Concern radiated from them, but they seemed content to let me talk. Good. Because I didn't know if

I could get through this story if they tried asking too many questions.

"You know I've shuffled around—"

"Sera," Brooks interrupted me.

My fingers scraped along the soft material of the couch as my chest tightened. Please. Not now.

He shook his head and moved to join me on the couch. "You don't have to do this."

I swallowed hard and tightened my resolve. "I need to."

He laced our fingers together.

Squeezing his hand, his touch gave me the strength to continue. "I've never had any kind of family."

Both Souta and JJ looked like they wanted to ask questions at my statement, but a slight shake of Brooks' head stopped them.

"I don't know why, but May always had trouble finding places for me to stay, especially during the longer summer breaks." Of course, eventually my reputation didn't help. "It was rare that I stayed with anyone for more than a couple weeks, and for the most part, I was left to my own devices. The classmates I stayed with were never close and rarely friends. I didn't really want them to be, either. The families were nice, polite, but I was always a guest. An outsider. And it was always obvious."

"Seriously?" Souta whispered. "Nothing? Ever?"

Tears threatened as I shook my head. "Nothing I have clear memories of. There was a family, when I was really little, but I only have vague impressions. My one clear memory of them is…" I closed my eyes as the memory rose in my mind "… painful."

I didn't want to relive it, but I needed them to understand. No running meant no hiding, either.

The story of the rejected bunny spilled out.

When I started to shake, an arm wrapped around me and pulled me in tight. Souta and JJ were out of their seats like shots from a gun, both managing to somehow settle in and wrap me up.

"Did you ever try to look them up again?" JJ asked when the words finally halted.

I wiped my damp cheeks, a bit pissed for crying while telling them about Tara and Mark.

Again, I mutely shook my head and willed my voice to remain steady and calm. "Honestly, I buried the memory so deep I didn't remember it until we were here the first time."

"Maybe you should ask Maybelle?" Souta grabbed my hips and moved me into his lap as he spoke.

His chest moved against my side as he drew in a

deep breath and let out a tiny, almost inaudible sigh. It hit me then, like a brick, that he did it more for himself than me. When things got rough or serious over the last few weeks, he'd be more affectionate than normal, like he needed the contact to settle his mind and reassure himself.

"I don't want to bother May with my silly issues when she already has so much to do." Still, ever since remembering how I'd left Tara and Mark, it hovered in the back of my mind, hinting at things I didn't look too deeply into. Would I be able to move past it without a few answers? "Maybe. I'll think about it."

"When you're ready, beautiful." Brooks ran a finger down my cheek, and I leaned into the touch.

We sat in silence for a moment, and I let myself take comfort in being wrapped up in my boys, knowing it wouldn't last long.

"I still don't understand," JJ spoke up first, lifting his head from where he'd been leaning against my legs. "Why were you running from us? Is it only because it's all so new and strange?"

"She doesn't realize it." At the unexpected voice, I looked up to find my brother leaning against the wall. "But deep down, it's because she doesn't think she's worth keeping around."

My lungs seized up as the rightness of his

words settled in and destroyed the veil I'd kept on my feelings. Tara and Mark didn't want me. And despite May's attempts, neither did anyone else. No one even tried to include me, to make me feel like more than someone taking up a spare room for a few days. Not one person, until them.

"Sera?" Souta's worried tone made me aware of how still I'd gone.

"He's right." Unable to move, I didn't know how to react to this or what to do about it.

"And I sure as fuck didn't help matters." Ash crossed the room toward me.

JJ stood to prevent him from getting too close.

Ash simply nodded and backed off a step or two. "I didn't know any of this when we talked, but I owe you a bigger apology than I realized."

JJ's stiff stance relaxed, and he sank back down to the floor to lean against Souta and my legs.

"I was a complete ass, and I will make it up to you." Ash strode around the couch, reached over, and ruffled my hair. "Tell them the rest, Seraphina. I'll be in the kitchen if you need me."

"I still don't like him," Souta grumbled against my neck as Ash left.

I poked his cheek, so he'd look up at me and see

the serious expression on my face. "He's my brother, and he's not going anywhere."

"Sorry." Souta's face fell. "What did he mean, the rest?"

Unable to meet any of their gazes, I focused on my lap as I answered. "You guys may have noticed I've been a bit erratic lately. I didn't want any of you to regret our Iunctura, and I've never been someone people wanted to keep around. Somehow, I thought I needed to be different and tried to figure out what you guys wanted me to be. How you wanted me to act or dress or whatever. But you each seemed to expect someone different, then there were Souta's parents. They were so nice to let me stay, and I felt like I needed to be the perfect guest, and I didn't know how. Meeting all the expectations..." I trailed off, unsure how to voice my worries, when the abrupt press of lips cut off my internal babble.

Lost in my explanation, I didn't notice JJ move. His tongue softly licked at the seam of my mouth, and I opened to him. All thoughts of what I should say flew out of my head as our tongues danced.

When he pulled back and sank to the floor, I simply stared, dazed, trying to remember what I was saying.

JJ propped an arm on my knees, resting his head

on it. "You don't need to be anything but the amazing, beautiful woman you are, firefly, and we're sorry if we made you feel like you did."

"It wasn't you." I shook my head.

Souta sat up straight suddenly, nearly sending me toppling off his lap.

Brooks steadied me as my hands clutched Souta's shirt for balance.

Souta's hands slid around me, "Sorry, hot stuff. But was that what was going on the other night? When you left? My folks had just—" He didn't need to finish.

Ruefully, I nodded. "Yes. Kind of. It was more—everything—too much everything, and them wanting me to do your fancy family thing was like a... I don't know. It just suddenly felt like I was suffocating, and I had to get out of there to figure things out. That didn't go well obviously." I shrugged, unsure how to explain it all. "I... I'm not good at the family thing."

"I think you're better at the family thing than you realize." My head swiveled to look at Brooks, my mind stalling over his words. "You keep standing up to Souta about Ash being your brother, and you've forgiven him pretty quickly."

Uncertain how to respond, I shrugged. "After seeing him the second time, it didn't feel like Ash hated me. He'd only reacted to the situation as anyone might. Eventually, he calmed down, took the time to listen, and think and do the right thing. Nothing good comes easily after all."

So, why did I expect to fall easily into a relationship, like I had been born in it? I laughed at my own silliness in my head.

"Try not to be so hard on yourself." JJ spun around and rose to sit on his knees. "We know it's all new. It's just, I think I speak for all three of us here, the connection between us was instant, even before Iunctura. And now it's gotten so much stronger. We forget how new being part of a family is for you. Be patient with yourself and with us, okay?"

"Me too?" I needed to remember I didn't have to handle everything on my own anymore either. No more long, solitary walks to try to work through stuff.

Thinking of my walks reminded me of another talk that needed to happen. "Souta?"

He must have read my expression because he nodded. "I know. We should talk." We both looked at JJ and Brooks.

Brooks jerked his head toward the hall. "Go. Fill us in later, okay? We can't help if we don't know."

My sigh of relief matched Souta's own, and I slid off his lap. I didn't want to hide things from any of them, but I wasn't ready to fight things out in front of everyone either.

We went into the foyer, and I settled onto the steps, eyes tracking Souta as he paced. So much happened in the last couple days. Everything felt broken between us, and I didn't know where to start to fix it. Souta ran a hand through his hair as he spun to a stop. The pain shimmering in his eyes made my heart ache.

"I'm sorry, Sera." He shook his head. "I can't get the image of Dane holding you out of my head."

"When you found us, he was actually asking if he should call you."

Souta sank to the ground. "I'm an idiot."

"But you're my idiot." I tried to lighten his mood and let him know my feelings never changed.

"Am I?" Hunched in on himself, Souta peered up at me from under his dark hair. I sucked in a breath at his vacant expression. "After everything? Should I be? Apparently, I didn't learn my lesson the first time around."

"What do you mean?" I slid down the stairs, the need to wrap my arms around him overriding any other emotions. I'd never seen him like this.

"I did something similar to Brooks." He drew his legs up and buried his face in them. "Barely a week after Iunctura. Brooks had only been in town a short time, remember, and it was obvious almost from the start that he had a thing for Dane, but Dane is straight. The first time we went out, I asked him about it. That's when Iunctura happened, and we had this amazing experience.

"But his crush on Dane left me wondering about his feelings for me, whether or not there were any, to be honest. Then I spent the next week at school seeing him in the company of this other guy, not Dane. He wouldn't come to lunch, but I'd see them leave the library, or he'd tell me he couldn't see me after school, then he'd be walking down the hall with this other guy."

Chin propped on his knees, Souta's dark hair obscured his eyes. "After about four days, I lost my mind, cornered him in the hall with this other guy, and said all kinds of things that don't bear repeating. I made all these insane accusations. He just stood there and took it, and when I finally shut the hell up, he just said, 'done then?' and walked away with the other dude."

"I fell apart, and the whole thing nearly broke us. Took JJ to put us back together. He went and talked to Brooks. Turned out the guy was his partner on a project for class. Sound familiar?" Souta snorted. "I can't even stop from repeating the same mistakes. I'm the world's biggest idiot."

I wrapped my arms around him and dropped a kiss to his temple. "Idiot." Another kiss to his cheek. "Dancer." His arm. "Singer." His head again. "Ventus." I nudged his head up and pecked his lips. "No matter what you are, you're still mine. And Brooks feels the same, I'm sure. JJ, too."

"I'll try to do better," Souta whispered against my lips.

"Why do you react that way?" It felt so out of character for him.

Souta pulled back, uncurling, hands moving to my hips before he stilled and let them fall to his lap.

I knew what he wanted—needed—so I shifted, tossing my legs over his to settle in his lap.

He smiled, a soft, tiny imitation of his usual grin, and moved his hands to rest on my thighs. "My dad—"

My forehead scrunched up. What would his dad have to do with anything? "Your dad is nice."

Souta's fingers absently stroked my inner thigh, sending heat shooting through me and pooling at my core. "Tadashi Kurihara isn't my biological father."

Shocked, I tried to contain my reaction but couldn't stop from blinking rapidly.

"He adopted me years ago, shortly after he married my mom. My biological father was a total bastard. Though I didn't know it until the end."

It was hard to listen and not squirm under Souta's still stroking fingers. "Souta?"

His name came out as little more than a breath of air as I tried to get his attention, but his unfocused gaze told me he was miles, or maybe years, away. My heart sped up, and my muscles tried to tense, but I drew slow, even breaths and quietly wrapped my hand around his to still the wandering fingers.

This was really not the time.

"My biological dad was my hero. We were very close." He spoke absently, and I moved our hands from my thigh to the floor as I listened. "Then one day when I was nine, he took me for a 'man weekend' or some crap like that. What he called it didn't matter because it was a lie, anyway."

He paused, gaze unfocused. The desire to say something rose, but I didn't know what, and I didn't want to jar him out of his thoughts, so I stayed silent.

"We went to this vacation cabin we had. I remember being completely psyched. But about an hour after we got there, this woman showed up, and my dad told me to entertain myself for the weekend."

Souta's voice cracked, a frown pulling his full mouth down.

I ran my thumb over the back of his hand, offering what little comfort I could.

"I barely saw him that weekend, and it was pretty obvious what was going on. Especially since the woman only threw one of my dad's shirts on when they bothered to leave the bedroom. At the end of the weekend, on the ride home, he went on this long spiel about how this was just between us men, Mom didn't need to know, and a bunch of other stuff I tuned out. It took less than a week for me to tell Mom.

"When she confronted him, he came at me. Told me I was a worthless little fuck and wasn't good enough to be his kid. Turned out he'd been cheating on my mom for years and, often, had more than one side-piece. The betrayal tore me up. Even now, I keep waiting to catch Tadashi cheating, even though I know he's a good man."

Echoing footsteps made us both look up in time to see Michael walk into the hall. When he saw us on the floor, his eyebrows raised. "That can't be comfortable. What are you two doing out here, anyway?"

At his words, the numbness seeping into my rear

became obvious. I stood, brushing imaginary dust off my jeans. "Souta and I had some things we needed to work out."

Behind me, Souta stood, hand finding my waist.

"Sorry to interrupt, but Ash told me what happened at the park." At first, I froze, horrified Ash told him my personal issues, until the rest of his statement registered. "We need to report the attempted kidnapping. I'm going to put in a call to a friend at the Sheriff's Office, but I wanted you to be prepared."

My stomach clenched. I didn't want to relive what happened, but he was right, I needed to report what happened.

Souta's hand tightened at my waist. "Sir?"

Michael's attention shifted to Souta.

"I think we should call the Lex, instead. The guy who tried to take her was an Elementum."

Michael nodded. "I'll go make the call. And Seraphina?" My attention snapped back to him. "No hurry on that decision okay? The offer always stands."

My throat went dry when Souta stilled behind me as Michael left. "What decision?"

TWENTY-THREE

Souta spun me around, a suspicious glint in his eyes. "Sera? What's going on?"

"I'd rather tell you all together." I failed to meet his eyes but held his hand.

With everything going on, how would they feel about Michael's offer? Backing up a couple steps, I tugged at Souta and headed back into the living room where JJ and Brooks waited.

They looked up as we came back in, conversation stopping.

"Okay?" Brooks glanced between Souta and me.

We both nodded.

It still felt unsettled and unsure, but mending. Like always, Brooks sensed my emotions and rose. He wrapped his arms around me, pulled me into him and tilted my head up so I met his beautiful blue eyes. A blond curl fell into his face, and I pushed it back.

"Whatever it is, beautiful, we'll deal with it together. That's what family does, what couples do." He pressed his lips to mine, gentle and soft, undemanding.

With a sigh, I melted into him, every muscle finally relaxing for the first time in days. His lips parted, encouraging mine to open to him. Flutters assaulted my stomach, heat simmered just below the surface. His tongue played around my lips, licking them slow and lazy, before thrusting into my mouth to take his time exploring. I loved kissing Brooks. I could kiss him like this for days.

All too soon, the kiss ended, leaving me dazed. A gentle tug on my hand alerted me to the fact I was being led, but since I landed in a familiar lap, I didn't mind.

JJ's chuckle vibrated me. "Did you have to kiss her stupid?"

"Can't be helped. Just how I kiss." Brooks grinned, then grabbed Souta.

Minutes later, I giggled as Souta stood with a similar dazed expression on his face.

JJ laughed into my shoulder, his whole body shaking.

"Bet I can do better," he whispered into my ear.

I turned my head, willing to let him try, but Michael walked into the room at that moment, followed by two unfamiliar and official-looking individuals. Stiffening, I leaned into JJ as his arms came around me to squeeze me.

I didn't want to do this, but I needed to.

"Seraphina, sweetheart, this is Lex Quinn and Lex Braxton."

I licked my suddenly dry lips and waved a greeting while my gaze investigated the two men who would take my statement. Neither looked overly intimidating, thankfully. Similar in height, one was willow thin while the other spent plenty of time at the gym.

As they walked into the room, the thin one's eyes drifted down his partner's backside and settled on his rear. I bit back a grin at the idea of him having a thing for his partner. No way, just my imagination I was sure, but it put me a little more at ease.

I tapped JJ's arm, so he'd release me, then rose and held my hand out to the Lex.

The brick wall wrapped his hand around mine in a barely-there grip. A sense of calm and cool washed over me, telling me he was likely Aqua. I'd never met an Aqua this big before.

"Lex Braxton, miss." His voice rumbled through me.

As he released me, his partner stepped forward, wrapping my hand in a warm, firm grip.

We only held for a second because our hands sparked against each other. Weird. I never reacted to another Ignis like that. Another question to put on my list for May.

His brow furrowed as he released me. "Lex Quin, Miss Phoenix."

"Embers, actually," I replied, the mistake completely understandable.

Lex Quin's eyes widened and darted between Michael and me.

"Embers?" He stepped back, the motion involuntary. "But that's not…" Shaking his head, he smiled at me. "Never mind."

"Seraphina, do you want me to stay?" Concern covered Michael's face.

"How old are you, Miss Embers?" Lex Braxton asked in his rumble.

"Eighteen," I answered before directing my attention back to Michael—my dad. "I'm okay, Dad." I reached back, unsurprised when JJ's hand found mine immediately. "But I'd appreciate you staying."

Michael nodded and leaned against the wall, leaving the chairs for the Lex.

Settling back onto JJ's lap, I motioned to the two available chairs. "Please, sit."

Braxton nearly didn't fit, his wide, muscled bulk filling the chair completely.

Quin, on the other hand, curled into his chair with his legs tucked up and still had room to spare. "All right, Miss Embers, why don't you tell us what happened?"

Heat rose in my cheeks as I realized there was no way to tell the story without getting into personal details.

JJ's arm tightened around me, and he nuzzled the back of my neck, the short strands of red hair ruffling from his breath.

A rustle of movement from the side caught my attention. Brooks and Souta both rose from the couch and settled on either side of me. Souta pulled my feet into his lap, twisting me to sit sideways on JJ. Brooks pressed a hand to the small of my back.

Taking a deep breath, the story poured out.

"I was talking to"—how to describe Dane?—"a friend in the park, and Souta showed up. He and my friend had words, and while they did—"

"Ma'am," Braxton rumbled, "we need you to tell us everything, please."

Briefly, my eyes closed tight, hands sweating.

Brooks' arm joined JJ's around my waist, and Souta's fingers dug into my calf, massaging gentle circles.

"We had a fight, Sera and me," Souta spoke up. "She left. Not like left me, but left the house, just for a walk. She does that all the time when she's upset, but she's promised to try to—"

Lex Quin held up a hand to stop Souta's swift flow of words. My stomach fluttered, giddiness filling me at the return of my familiar, bubbly guy.

"I'm sorry, but are you both—" He looked at us, wrapped up together. "Are you all involved?"

"Well, we're all involved with her," JJ responded as he pressed a kiss to my cheek.

Michael chuckled. "They're her Genus."

Lex Quin nodded and waved his hand for Souta to continue.

"So, we had this fight, and my girl here took off, and about twenty seconds after she left, I realized I was being stupid and said shit I didn't mean. When I went after her, I found her talking to her friend, and they looked cozy." Souta stopped for a breath.

"Jealousy got the better of me, and I got in the guy's face."

"I got it, Souta." Laughter laced my voice. "So, Souta and Dane were fighting, when suddenly I was grabbed and pulled away from them. When I got a look at the guy, it clicked that we'd seen him before, at school, talking to Scholae Jones."

"Do you know who he was?" Braxton leaned forward.

"Chester Wyn," Souta replied.

Lex Braxton noted the name on the tablet I hadn't noticed before.

"How did you get away?" Lex Quin asked.

"I screamed for Souta. I'm a heater, and I tried heating my skin, but it didn't seem to bother him. Souta saw us and sent wind gusts, but they didn't seem to bother him, either." I hesitated, not wanting to report the next bit but knowing it was impossible not to.

While Dane might be a jerk, he did seem to be trying to be better, and I didn't want to get him in trouble.

"Then this gust— I don't even think that's a good word for it. This wind"—I shook my head, words failing me—"stronger than anything I've ever felt, barreled through and tore us apart. Chester left after that."

"I've only felt the kind of wind that happened in the most advanced Elementum," Souta said. "It came from our direction. I was still throwing my power out, and I think the guy she was talking to, Dane, threw his out, too. I can't do anything that strong on my own."

It still struck me as odd since, during training at school, multiple powers were often being thrown around at the same time, and nothing like that ever happened.

Lex Quin met Lex Braxton's eyes; a silent conversation took place. "Okay, thank you. What is Dane's last name? We'll need to get a statement from him."

"Hicks," I replied. "During the week he lives in the dorms at Illustratio."

I didn't know if they needed that detail, but it couldn't hurt to save them the step of tracking him down.

With their questions over, they rose and shook our hands again.

Michael paced over to the doorway. "Gentleman, I'll show you out."

They nodded in passing before they left.

Hopefully, I'd never see them again. With a sigh, I sank into the chair Lex Quin recently vacated and waited.

Souta sat on the couch, raised an eyebrow. "Sera?"

Knowing what he wanted, my fingers found my cuticles and started picking. "So, there's something I should tell you, and I don't know how you're all going to feel about it." My eyes found a spot on the floor and fixated there. I didn't want to see their expressions when I told them. "Michael and Kelly have asked me to come stay with them."

Silence hung heavy in the air, no one even shifting. A finger under my chin startled me, and I jumped back in the chair.

JJ's gaze greeted me. "Firefly, do you want to stay with them?"

"I don't…" I stumbled over my words as my gaze drifted to Souta. "I don't know."

He sat stiffly, spine straighter than I'd ever seen it.

"Souta?" Fear skittered through me at his continued silence, and his unusual stillness.

JJ's hand drifted down and tangled with my own.

Finally, Souta's dark eyes lifted to meet my own. "Did I do something wrong?" His voice cracked. "I mean, I know I did, but I swear I'll do better, Sera, I promise."

I gave JJ a gentle nudge to move him aside, and he shifted to let me stand. Closing the distance between us in a few short strides, I crawled into Souta's lap, pried his clenched hands apart, and wrapped them around me. Lightly, I pressed kisses along his neck, trailed up to his jaw, then pressed a short, swift one to his lips.

"I think I do want to stay, but it's nothing against you." While JJ and Brooks didn't look happy, they didn't look unhappy, either. "Nothing against any of you." I turned back to Souta, making sure he met my eyes. "It's nothing against your parents, either. They're great, honest. I mean, not everyone would let some girl they only just met come live with them because of their son."

I watched his face carefully. He needed to understand this wasn't his fault. "I'm still not comfortable living with them, true, but that's not anything to do with me staying here."

He nodded, a smile lifting the corner of his mouth.

"I want to stay because he's my dad. I've dreamed of real parents my entire life, even if I never admitted it to myself. And he's here. I want this. I want to spend time with him and Ash and Kelly. I want that experience. But Souta, you, JJ, and Brooks— You're my home, too, no matter where I live."

Souta's mouth came down hard on my own before the words entirely left me. A quick, hard press, over as swiftly as it began. Before I could register what happened, hands tugged me over until I found myself in Brooks' lap with more kisses being delivered.

When I plopped down into JJ's lap and received another quick kiss, I pushed against his chest, laughing. "Stop passing me around like I'm a turkey, guys!"

Seriously, they were being ridiculous. They could all have simply leaned over to where I already sat.

"You're most definitely not a turkey." JJ squeezed me. "You're our beauty."

"Our heart," Brooks chimed in.

"Our passion," Souta finished off.

My insides warmed, and a silly grin stole over my face. "This has to be the cheesiest, most ridiculous moment ever."

I never thought for a moment I would ever be part of something straight out of a novel. Even still, I smiled so wide I thought it might break my face.

A throat clearing got our attention, and I looked up to find Michael standing in the doorway with an unexpected guest.

May smiled and breezed into the room with a sure step.

A blush crept up my neck and over my cheeks, warming my skin as I crawled off JJ's lap. For a moment, I debated whether to stay on the floor or take a seat on the couch, but decided it likely didn't matter.

May settled into the chair I had recently vacated. "I hear we have some things to talk about."

TWENTY-FOUR

"Your father filled me in." May's deep brown eyes filled with concern as she assessed me. "Come here." She waved me over, and I stood to cross the room and stand in front of her. "Let me look you over. Did he hurt you? Use any power on you?"

I held out my arms for her inspection. "No. He never even hinted at what element he was. His grip was firm but not hard enough to bruise."

May took hold of my left hand and turned my arm around before doing the same to the other, before releasing my hand and sitting back. "And who was it?"

"Chester Wyn," Souta answered for me.

His need to pull me back into his lap was etched

into every adorable line on his face. His fist clenched tight as his side. I wouldn't sit in any laps with May here, but I moved and took a seat in between him and Brooks, pulling his tightly clenched fist into my lap and twisting our fingers together.

May pursed her lips in thought. "Doesn't ring any bells, but I'll look into him. Now, you have questions?"

My stomach fluttered. "I had a memory." The words caught in my throat, but I pushed them out. "A terrible memory." Throat still tight, my eyes began to burn. "There were two people, Mark and Tara, and they didn't… didn't want me anymore. You had to take me away…"

Wetness streaked down my cheek, and I realized I'd begun to cry.

"Oh, darling." May rose and closed the distance between us. She crouched, gathered me into her arms, and held me close for a moment before releasing me. "You were too young to understand, then you didn't seem to remember any of it. I should have talked to you about it years ago."

She settled back into the chair before continuing. "When you were five, Tara found out she was pregnant."

"And then she didn't want me anymore," I finished the statement for her.

May shook her head. "No, honey. She couldn't take care of you. Tara loved you very much. So did Mark."

It was hard to believe her, but I wanted to, so I stayed quiet.

"They tried for years to have children, but Tara couldn't maintain a pregnancy. When your mom died, I knew she'd be thrilled to take you in. She wanted to adopt you, but the rest of the Concilium wanted to wait. When she got pregnant, her doctor told her she needed to be extra cautious. She tried, for about three months, but she had a scare, and her doctor put her on bed rest. That's when she called me. She wasn't able to take care of an active five-year-old."

Time slowed down around me as my reality readjusted. For weeks, well years if I was honest, I thought Tara gave me up because she simply didn't want me anymore, because I was too much trouble or work. But May said Tara did want me, that she loved me? I barely registered the arm pulling me close.

"It broke her heart to tell me. She hoped to be able to get you back after the baby was born, but her health became very delicate. She asked about you for years. Wanted to know everything about you." The way her eyes suddenly went sad made my heart fall.

"May?" Please don't say it. "Could I talk to her?"

Please don't let it be true. Don't say it.

"I'm sorry, darling. She died several years ago."

More tears escaped me. Tara loved me. My brain couldn't wrap itself around that.

Silence filled the room, but I couldn't do anything more than curl into Brooks and cry silently.

May rubbed my back. "Mark would love to see you. He still asks about you. When you're ready, honey."

I nodded. I did want to see him, talk to him. Eventually.

Michael added quietly, "We would be happy to set up a dinner or lunch, if they live in state."

"Beautiful," Brooks whispered. "What about the power surge?"

Thankful for the reminder, I wiped my eyes looked back up at May. Tears still glistened in her eyes.

"Something odd happened during training." I swallowed down a sob and tried to continue. "I didn't mean to, but somehow my power surged or something, and I burned Souta badly. I didn't... I don't have that much power. I've never been able to do anything like that before, but it's happened twice."

May stayed silent for several minutes.

I snuggled into Brooks and settled my feet in Souta's lap. My hand found JJ's hair and ran through it. Physical connection to my boys was what I needed right now. The mystery still bothered me, but I had put the surge out of my mind, especially when I'd been unable to find any answers in the Tabularium.

After a few minutes of contemplation, May rose. "I have some ideas on the matter, but I'm not entirely sure. Let me look into it." She gathered her purse to head out, and I rose, too. "I don't want to give you false information, sweetie."

I walked her to the door, grateful again the Mother saw fit to give me such an incredible guardian.

At that moment, standing by the door with the one woman who always stood by my side, it hit me how much I'd taken her for granted. Without thinking about it, I threw my arms around her and hugged her tight.

Her shock froze her for a second, then she enfolded me in her arms.

"May, I'm so sorry." The urge to tell her how I felt came out. She'd been the one steady presence in my life since the day I was born. "I've taken you for granted for so long." My throat closed again, and I cursed this new tendency to cry at the drop of a hat.

"Oh, child." May ran a hand over my hair. "I don't think that's true."

"But it is." I pulled back to look at her. "I never realized, I never thought…" My words failed, and for half a second, panic overtook me. Pausing, I forced a deep breath and tried again, "I've spent years thinking I was alone in the world, and the whole time you were there, in the background. Every time I called, every holiday. You've always been there for everything. I was never alone, and I failed to see it."

"Child, don't you know how much I love you? I've always thought of you as one of my grandchildren. Family is there for each other, without question and without thanks needed." Her hands squeezed mine. "And it doesn't matter that you have the boys, Michael, Kelly and Ash now. I will still be only a phone call away."

"I've still been an idiot." I gave her half a smile and shoved some hair out of my face.

"No, Sera. Not an idiot. What you've been is hurt and growing up." She leaned in and pecked my cheek. "I have to go, but I expect phone calls, hear?"

"I will." I nodded.

My heart felt like it would burst from happiness as I watched her walk out the door.

A hand came down gently on my shoulder and squeezed. Looking back, I found Michael standing there. "I didn't mean to eavesdrop, but she's right, you know. Family doesn't ask for thanks or even acknowledgment. They are simply there because of love."

"I think I'm starting to understand that." Closing the door, I turned to face him. "And I wanted to tell you that I accept your offer. If it's still okay, I would love to come live with you."

The grin practically broke his face, and I didn't bother to stop my answering one. The roller coaster I'd been on the last few days left me a little lightheaded, but I didn't mind. It felt better than being nearly numb for the last eighteen years.

"Come on, then." He jerked his head toward the living room where the boys still waited. "Why don't we go figure out some house rules with your boys?"

This should be interesting. What kind of rules would he set down?

The boys looked up from the couch when we walked in, questions all over their faces. I went over and tossed myself down in the middle of them, making them laugh as they tried to rearrange us into a more comfortable pile.

"Alright, guys." Michael laughed as we settled. "With Seraphina's agreement to live here, I think we need to establish a few rules. You are all welcome anytime, but absolutely no closed doors, okay?"

"Seriously, Dad?" Ash snorted as he walked in. "That's it? No closed doors?"

He spun to face the guys, and I bit back a laugh at the expression on his face. It was a cross between fierce older brother and class clown, which really shouldn't work.

"That's my little sister." He thrust a finger at me. "How about this rule?" He turned toward me and the guys. "Remember she's got an older brother who won't hesitate to kick your asses and let that guide you."

It was a battle to hold in the laughter bubbling up in my chest. Ash knew I could take care of myself, but I rather enjoyed having him in my corner.

Michael didn't bother holding in his chuckle as he clapped a hand down on Ash's shoulder. "A curfew will be set, but we'll figure out the rest of the rules as we go. It will take a little adjusting for all of us."

Kelly came in with a tray of snacks, smiling as she set it on the coffee table and settled into a chair. I still didn't know her well, but that would change with me living here. I wasn't sure what kind of role she'd have in my life, but she was important to Michael, so she was important to me.

It hit me then, how many people I now had who were important to me, who mattered, who I cared for. It felt new and odd, and I was still adjusting, but with the guys' help, I would figure things out.

And Chester, and the power surges? We would figure all that out, too.

We had plenty of help now, plenty of people in our corner. Answers would come in time.

Nick and Riley seem destined for each other, if only they realized their mutual attraction.

Computer tech geek, Nick, can't seem to kick his crush on his straight neighbor, Riley. After six months of living next door to each other, he finally accepts his best friend's offer to set him up on a date to get over his unrequited love.

Angel Falls detective, Riley, just came out of a bad relationship and isn't ready to risk his heart again. But he can't help the feelings developing for his neighbor, Nick, or the push from his partner to confess his attraction. Everything changes, though, after he sees Nick with a new guy, and Riley realizes he may have hidden his feelings too well, costing him a chance with the man he loves.

Despite Nick's new relationship, Riley can't deny the feeling that every time they're near each other, the air seems to sizzle. Is Nick not as committed to his new boyfriend as Riley thinks?

When Nick is attacked his apartment, will it be the final push to bring them together? Or will it drive them apart?

ABOUT THE AUTHOR

Desi Lin lives in Central Florida with her husband, four kids, and one spoiled, pure black kitty. She enjoys a good cup of coffee, a great tune and delicious food. When not writing, she can be found cooking, taking photographs, playing on her Xbox and driving her kids nuts.

Made in the USA
Columbia, SC
23 January 2023

75756577R00183